CHILD TRAFFICKING AND THE UNDERGROUND RAILROAD

BRYAN MOSHER

Copyright © 2024 by Bryan Mosher

All rights reserved.

No part of this book may be reproduced in any form or by any electronic or mechanical means, including information storage and retrieval systems, without written permission from the author, except for the use of brief quotations in a book review. For permission contact Bryan Mosher at Bryanmosher.writes@gmail.com.

Beta readers: Mary Jane Dennis, Carolyn McNeese, Mary Ellen Johnston

Editing by Mary Ellen Johnston and Mary Jane Dennis

Cover Artwork by Natasha Sazonova

Formatting by Lynessa Layne

Hardcover ISBN 978-1-956848-39-7

Paperback ISBN 978-1-956848-37-3

eBook ISBN 978-1-956848-38-0

I dedicate this book to my wife of 41 years Judy without whom I could not have attained my achievements.

*My three children, Brandon, Brian, and Jennifer who have become good productive citizens, role models,
and parents despite their father's influence.*

*My seven grandchildren who always seem
to be able to put a smile on my face.*

Anyone fighting Cancer and Alzheimer's two horrific diseases.

*Jesus Christ my lord and savior who has given me the opportunity not
once but several times to pursue my dreams.*

*And, last but not least, to the children and families that have had to
deal with child trafficking firsthand, the law enforcement who are on the
front lines battling this horrific crime, and the public who chooses not to
turn a blind eye. See something say something.*

PREFACE

Behind every novel is an idea, a spark, a reason to tender that spark into a flame. A flame that catches the attention of a novelist that starts a fire in his soul. This novel is no different. There were two sparks that started a fire in this author's soul, and they came about within days of one another.

The first was an attempted child abduction from a nearby Walmart. The second was a discussion with a friend of mine refurbishing an old civil war era home. They found a secret room and believe it was used as part of the underground railroad. Taking those two occurrences it seemed like the perfect way to combine the past and the present.

Is there anymore critical law enforcement and public outcry than to stop child trafficking and stop it now. I hope this novel demonstrates how it can be taking place right under our noses and when the community works with law enforcement it can be stopped.

INTRODUCTION

Many people believe that it can't happen, that it can't happen here, in the United States. A U.S. Department of State 2019 Trafficking Persons Report, states that 77 percent of trafficking victims are exploited within their country of residence.

The National Human Trafficking Hotline statistics show a 25 percent jump in human trafficking cases from 2017 to 2018. This includes sex and labor trafficking. Of the more than 23,500 runaways reported to the National Center for Missing and Exploited Children in 2018, 1 in 7 were likely victims of child sex trafficking.

Child Trafficking occurs all over the world. The United States is one of the most active sex trafficking countries in the world. Exploitation of trafficking victims occurs in cities, suburban, and rural areas. Many people assume most trafficking victims in the U.S. are undocumented immigrants. Most domestic trafficking victims are U.S. citizens.

Although this novel is a work of fiction, the fact is, we have a serious problem in this country. This story was prompted by a child abduction from a store parking lot just a mile from my home. That same thing could be happening in your backyard too.

The methods used to move its victims from one secret location to the next is paramount. Keeping the movement of the victims secret was essential to the continued operation and profitability of the endeavor. Methods of movement were varied and imaginative. What better way than to adopt a proven method used over one hundred and fifty years ago, THE UNDERGROUND RAILROAD.

When a victim is rescued from an old underground railroad station this grandfather, his two grandsons, local law enforcement, and concerned citizens just like you can no longer sit on the sidelines. Time for this railroad to be derailed.

This novel tells how a senior citizen, two ten-year-old boys, a doctor, and law enforcement, come together to expose and shutdown a child trafficking ring, utilizing the underground railroad in exploiting children.

PROLOGUE

Due to my parents splitting up when I was five years old, I grew up in my grandfather's home. My grandparents played a vital role in my upbringing.

I was a very fortunate boy. Rarely further than an arms distance from him he ended fielding no less than 10,000 questions a day. He never failed to try and answer them all.

In this novel I have tried to portray my grandfather in almost a heroic light and I can assure you he was that and more. So much can be learned from the previous generation, don't let that knowledge fail to be passed down.

Too soon it will be lost forever.

PART I

CHAPTER 1

It was summer vacation and like thousands of kids all over the country ten-year-old Kathy Sweet and her parents were moving. They were leaving their home in Phoenix, Arizona and moving to Prattville, Alabama. Despite what her dad said, this was going to be a boring ride. Why wouldn't her parents let her stay home like her older brother's, at least until her mom and dad found a new house. They were moving her away from relatives, her school, and her friends. She knew she would never fit in with those southerners. What could ever make this trip not boring?

In Prattville, Alabama two ten-year-old boys were dropped off with their grandparents for the summer. Their grandfather had a deal worked out with their parents that when their children turned 10, they would spend the summer with them.

The two cousins would give anything to stay home for the summer. In Illinois, Harry was the star pitcher for his little league team and in Virginia, Shane was winning most of the 5K races that he entered. Both their rooms were quickly being filled with trophies and medals. Both boys felt their time would be better spent at home increasing their skills in their chosen sports. No matter what arguments were made, their parents would not be swayed. The boys were told this was only one summer and it had a huge impact on their education.

It turns out these three ten-year-old children would get quite the education indeed. Little did they know they will get educated this summer in the subject of **Child trafficking.**

Both LeRoy and Judy had the benefits of having their grandparents living next door while they grew up. They knew that grandparents played a vital role in the education and exposure to life lessons.

Several years ago, a deal was struck between the grandparents and their children that when each of the 7 grandchildren turned ten years of age, they would each spend the entire summer with them. A promise was made by the grandparents that the stay would be educational and make up for the fact that all of the grandchildren lived a twelve-hour drive away. In return for the grandchildren's spending the summer with the grandparents each child would receive a 10,000-dollar scholarship to the college or trade school of their choice.

As grandparents, they knew that by spending the summer with them, they would get a lot more out of it than a mere 10,000 dollars. Both LeRoy and Judy had the benefits of having the benefits of grandparents living next door and knew that grandparents played a vital role in the education and exposure to life lessons. It was their desire to teach those same life lessons to their grandchildren.

Their children were dead set against leaving their children with the grandparents for an entire summer vacation, but the 10,000 dollars for college was too important to turn down.

Two years ago, when grandchildren Bianca and Jack had turned 10, they had been the first to spend the summer with their grandparents. During their stay they had been transformed. They were not the same 10-year-old kids that they had sent. They came back more respectful, more grown up, and more focused than the kids they had dropped off just 2 months earlier. That summer stay turned into an adventure they will remember for the rest of their lives. While at the Montgomery, Alabama History Museum with their grandfather they discovered a document that led to the

Child Trafficking and the Underground Railroad

discovery of the Confederate submarine the Hunley. Despite the death of all three crews aboard the Hunley it had the honor of being the first submarine. The Hunley had gone missing in 1864 following an attempt to sink a northern wooden hulled ship, blockading the Southern port of Charleston, South Carolina. The two grandchildren and the research they had done led to the discovery of the sunken submarine. Resulting in national recognition, a meeting with the governor of South Carolina, and a key to the city of Charleston. The discovery resulted in an in-person interview on Fox and Friends as well as many other awards for the role they played leading to the discovery of the Hunley.

Both Jack and Bianca now have a thirst for education and especially for history that they never had before. The parents of the kids compared notes and found that each of the kids had become "A" students since being left with the grandparents for the summer. They had been contacted by the "Save the Hunley Foundation" and they and their families were invited to Charleston for a special tour of the Hunley, its restoration, and the new museum.

This year it was two grandsons turns to spend the summer with the grandparents. Shane from Gloucester, Virginia, and Harrison, (Harry), from Mascoutah, Illinois would both be joining the grandparents in Prattville, Alabama. Of course, no one expected they would have anywhere near the adventure of their older siblings. Then again, stranger things have happened.

Neither of the boys were happy about the plans for the summer. Harry was going to miss the majority of baseball season where he was likely to have been the starting pitcher for his team, and Shane was going to miss four 5K races that he was planning on finishing among the top runners.

Harry's parents tried to make the decision easier to swallow by telling him that the grandparents planned on taking them to a triple A baseball game of the Montgomery, Biscuits. They were reminded that their grandfather had a friend who was the manager and would introduce them to the players and show them the locker room before a game.

Harry felt sad by not being able to pitch this summer but was looking forward to meeting the Biscuit Baseball Players and maybe add to his autograph collection would make the summer bearable.

Shane's parents told Shane that his grandfather had shared with them that he had scheduled some one-on-one time with the college track coach from the University of Auburn. Although he was looking forward to meeting the track coach it wasn't the same as running in the 5K races back home and winning medals.

These added bonuses were barely enough to pacify both boys, however, they still had concerns it was going to be boring hanging around with their grandparents all summer.

As agreed, both families would arrive on Saturday June 22. As promised when the 22nd of June arrived so did the families. As soon as the cars were parked in the driveway all seven grandchildren ran into the house, said their hello's, changed into their bathing suits, and hit the pool in the backyard.

The only one more excited than the grandchildren heading to the pool was Abby the six-year-old black Labrador Retriever. Unfortunately for Abby she was not allowed to join the kids in the pool. She had a habit of jumping in and retrieving them if they went underwater. She was very protective, and for some reason thought that anyone swimming underwater was in danger. She would retrieve them and bring them. She did this by grabbing onto their bathing suits and bringing them to the surface. More than one bathing suit had gone into the rag bin due to this natural habit of hers.

CHAPTER 2

While the kids splashed in the pool the parents unloaded the cars. Judy, the grandmother, handed out sleeping assignments while Le Roy, the grandfather, as usual, was nowhere to be found.

Harry's mom, Jennifer, asked, "where's Dad?"

"With his new toy in the garage, the old fool has got himself a new grill, something called a pellet grill. Supposed to be the latest and greatest. You know your father; he must try and improve on everything," she said. "You better prepare yourself; he says he is cooking dinner for all of us on that newfangled grill of his. Don't worry I have the pizza place on speed dial."

"Now Mom," Jennifer replied, "you know as well as I do, Dad has ALWAYS been a pretty good cook."

"Yes, I know, but he must know how every little thing works. It is the engineer in his blood. I had hoped that his twenty years in the Navy and twenty-four with General Electric would have gotten all of that out of his system. Do you know he almost missed church on Sunday because he had taken the control box of that grill apart and wanted to put it back before he forgot how it went back together," she laughed.

"We aren't getting any younger you know. Having the grandkids here for the summer will take years off the old coot. He has been planning this summer's adventure for months."

"What is this year's adventure Shane's mother, Angela, asked?

"Lord if I know. That man can keep secrets better than the CIA or the FBI," she replied. "Maybe you can get it out of him?"

Harry's dad Aaron, the son in law, and Shane's dad Brandon, the son, headed to the garage where the grandfather was standing before his pellet grill. The most wonderful smells were of smoking meat were coming out of the smokestack.

Immediately they could tell that the grill had been modified. Brandon chuckled as some memories of his dad's past modifications he had made. His father "often called improvements" had been made over the years. He must admit many of his modifications did make an improvement, but when they failed, they failed big time. He shared with Aaron the time his dad had driven a stake into the center of the back yard. Then he had attached two ropes to the self-propelled mower. What was supposed to happen was that the mower was supposed to wind itself around the stake and with each pass as more and more rope got wound around the stake it would cut smaller and smaller circles until the whole lawn was mowed.

"What happened?" Aaron asked.

Brandon said, "It was a good idea and it worked until the third time the mower went around the stake. The knot I had tied either came undone or the rope broke. The mower took off and ran over mom's tulip bed. She was one very mad woman. Dad never blamed me for tying a bad knot. He took full blame. For the next two weeks we spent two hours every night tying navy knots. I think I can still tie a bowline in my sleep."

Aaron and Brandon both had a good laugh.

"Okay Dad how have you "improved" your pellet grill?" Brandon asked.

"All the improvements I have made so far have been in the hopper area. This pellet grill was one of the less expensive grills on the market. I wanted to see if it was as advertised—*A new way to smoke and cook all in one*—before I invested a lot of money into it. As I researched it, I discovered that the difference between the expensive pellet grills and the less expensive models is the expensive models are made of thicker metal which only comes into play if you are grilling when it is cold outside. That and the hopper. The size of the hopper determines how long you can cook without having to add more pellets. I have overcome that obstacle by adding the funnel that extends the length of the hopper for another 8 ". That allows me to add all the pellets I need so I can feed it all the fuel to do the long cooks like pork shoulders or beef brisket.

Some of the cooks are 12 hours or more. Without this improvement I would have to stop what I was doing and add more pellets to the hopper. Another feature that is helpful is having a dump door on the hopper to quickly remove all the pellets. I haven't installed that yet. As you can see there are four 5-gallon buckets and all of them contain a different seasoned pellet. For instance, because I am cooking a pork tenderloin, I am using apple wood pellets. If I was doing a beef roast, I might choose a hickory or mesquite pellet. The dump feature allows me to change from one flavor pellet to another in minutes instead of hours."

Aaron said, "That is all very interesting but when are we going to eat? I'm starving."

"We should be able to eat in about a half hour," I said. "Go tell the women to set the table on the deck, we can watch the kids swim while we eat in peace. The kids can eat later after they have had a chance to burn off some of the energy they stored up from the long drive."

CHAPTER 3

They all sat down to eat some of the wonderful pork tenderloin that I had cooked on my pellet grill and from the look on their faces and the lack of conversation it was out of this world.

After dinner the conversation at the table turned to the subject of child trafficking here in Prattville that had recently made the national news.

My daughter, Jennifer said, "I heard it was especially bad here in Prattville due to its location near two major interstates."

"That's right," I said, "Interstate 65 which runs from the Florida / Alabama state line all the way to Chicago, Illinois and Interstate 85 which runs from Montgomery, Alabama through Atlanta, Georgia and then on to Richmond, Virginia."

"That's just horrible," Angela said.

"Dad," Jennifer said, "You must promise me you will watch over the boys while they are in your care. I don't know what I would do if somebody took one of my boys. Why can't people do something about this?"

Brandon added, "I read that it has reached epidemic proportions."

Soon the kids realized there was food, and they were missing out.

They descended on the table like locusts on a field of corn. Wet, dripping pool water, and ravenous.

"You would swear we never feed them," Angela said with a laugh.

I told them after supper and some more pool time, I would light the fire pit and we could all make s'mores for dessert. The dads joined in the pool and there was a lot less pool water after the big kids got done splashing the little kids and vice versa.

As promised, I got the fire-pit going and retrieved the marshmallow roasting forks from the shed. Soon there were marshmallows toasting. Some a nice golden brown while others were aflame and looked like a meteor entering earth's atmosphere from outer space. The problem with s'mores is there is no way to eat them without getting all that sticky marshmallow stuff all over you. I watched the kids eat their s'mores and my kids eat theirs and I was ready to make one for myself when I looked up and my wife was closely watching me to see that no graham cracker melted marshmallow or Hershey's chocolate entered my lips. Ever since my doctor warned me that I was approaching type 2 diabetes she had been watching me like a hawk. I tried to explain that just one s'more wouldn't hurt and that is when She gave me THE LOOK.

Then it was pajama time and the kids gathered around for me to tell them what it was like growing up in the olden days. Telling stories is one of the things I enjoy most. Two stories and all the kids headed up the stairs. With no complaints because after 3 hours in the pool with their cousins and consuming enough food to fill the shelves of a small grocery store had really worn them out.

The kids were settled into bed and the adults were gathered in the living room the topic of conversation again turned into what could be done to stop kids from being kidnapped and ending up in the child trafficking pipeline.

Ideas were exchanged back and forth but at the end we were no closer to a solution. We did come to the conclusion that it would have to be a joint effort with law enforcement, politicians, the press, and the public working together.

The next morning the families were up early and packed up for their journeys back home. Hugs and kisses were shared. Everyone agreed on a reunion date of August 7th which allowed time for Shane and Harry to get their school prep done. Stuff like buying school supplies and new clothes to start the new year. Shane and Harry were given extra big hugs from their families. Leaving them in the care and protection of their grandparents for the next two months was going to be difficult for most of them.

Time for the adventures to begin.

CHAPTER 4

The first day with me both boys couldn't wait to see what was on the agenda. Morning started with a few chores a hearty breakfast of pancakes, sausage, and maple syrup. Then hopping in my quad door ram pickup truck and we took off to the capital city of Montgomery, Alabama.

I told them that when I was a young boy just about your age my grandfather used to play a game with me that I would later use many times to my advantage. The boys wanted to know what kind of game, both said they liked games. It starts with a game that I am sure you have played, "I spy something". Then you are given a clue like a color, and you try to guess what it is by naming everything you can see that is that color. When you guess it then it becomes your turn to choose something for the other person to guess.

Shane said, "I used to play that with my sister, but she cheats. I would guess what she was thinking of and then she would change what it was so I wouldn't get a turn."

The game I have in mind is quite a bit harder. It isn't so much what you see but what you remember seeing.

For example, over the next couple months we will have driven over the same roads numerous times. I might ask a question like how many fast-food restaurants did we pass, and can you name them? Or what side of the road were they on, or can you name them in order? What this does is train your brain.

The boys chuckled over that one. If you think about it your eyes see everything, but unless your brain is trained, it remembers very little of what your eyes have seen.

Why is that important the boys wanted to know? It is so important that law enforcement classes teach this almost from day one of their training classes. At the police academy they run several exercises, often interrupting the scheduled class. Let me give you an example. Right in the middle of a class someone walks in carrying a fake gun and robs the instructor of his wallet. He then exits the room; he might be there one minute, at the most two. After he leaves, the trainees are asked to write down everything they remember about the robber. In the beginning of their training, they don't do very well. Just as many of the trainees said that the robber was tall as said he was short. Some people say he had on a coat of various colors, and some said he didn't have on a coat. Some said his gun was a revolver and others said it was an automatic. Some even said he wore a hat and an argument started over what kind of hat he had wore. They get asked to identify what was stolen from the instructor and most said it was either a dark brown or black wallet.

Then the officer who had acted as the robber came into the room and they got to really look at him. He was neither tall nor short. He didn't have on a coat but instead wore a navy sweatshirt with the fighting Irish logo on the front and no hat was on his head. His gun was neither a revolver nor an automatic but turned out to be an over ripe banana his wife had packed in his lunch earlier in the week. The wallet you ask was it black or brown? No hat was on his head. Turns out it wasn't a wallet at all but our instructors ham sandwich on rye his wife had packed in his lunch that morning. The instructor asked for his sandwich back and the pretend robber said he was sorry, but the ham sandwich was a casualty and was now evidence and couldn't be returned. As you can imagine the entire class was rolling on the floor laughing.

During the training at the academy several exercises like this take place, some actual live demonstrations and many more video clips. The trainees hone their skills and soon are not mistaking a banana for a gun. They can identify a suspect's height within an inch and their weight within a couple of pounds. I am sure you can see how important that is in a police officer's line of work.

The officers were quick to realize that an untrained eye is just that untrained. Every trainee in that room saw the exact same thing but, can you imagine putting out a "be on the lookout for bulletin" that had all those wrong answers. Police officers often must make a split-second decision on what they just saw. It could mean the difference between life and death. I can't think of a single skill that is more important in any job than this one.

That same skill set is a valuable tool in every line of work. A baseball coach needs to know when his pitcher has thrown enough pitches, a distance runner needs to identify any potholes in his path, so he doesn't turn an ankle. So why is it important to know what your eyes have seen?

My grandsons decided to put me through the test and asked me what was in the store front window of the National Auto store we just drove past.

I said, "What caught your eye? Was it the red bicycle, the blue bicycle, or maybe the sign that said free kittens, ask inside."

"Holy cow!" the boys exclaimed. "It really works."

CHAPTER 5

We had an appointment with the track coach at AUM, (Auburn University at Montgomery). We drove to the field house and met the track coach. I introduced them to the coach at the college. His name was Patrick Hilgendorf. When the boys both heard his last name, they chuckled.

Coach Hilgendorf told the boys, "You can just call me Coach H."

The coach wanted to watch the way Shane ran, and he said, "As long as he is here, let's watch your other grandson run as well."

Harry was quick to join in.

Coach H had them each do some warmup exercises before running.

He told them, "It is very important to do warmup exercises before and cooldown exercises after every sporting event.

"For some sports it is more important than others and running sports more than most. If you fail to warmup or cooldown properly it can cause injury and you won't perform at your peak."

He had them do toe touches, jumping jacks, running in place, and various stretches.

He then had them each run 100 meters telling them it was not a race, but of course two ten-year-old boys quickly made it one. Not surprising Shane won, but not by much.

Coach H then had them do cooldown exercises by walking at a normal pace once around the track. When the boys got back to the starting point the coach led us back into the field house. We followed him into a classroom, and he started a video projector. We watched a college athlete run; Coach H put it in slow motion so we could see every move he made.

Coach H said, "That is Jim, the captain of the track team. He is a world class distance runner.

He pushed a button on the projector and the screen we were watching split in two. The new side of the screen showed Shane and Harry both running.

"Hey that's us," both boys shouted in unison.

And sure enough, there they were looking like they were racing the college track star.

"Okay boys," the coach said. "Do you see any differences between the way you are running, and the way Jim is running?"

Shane spoke up, "His arms are going a lot higher than mine and Harry's."

"Very good observation Shane," coach replied.

Not to be outdone, Harry pointed out, "He appears to be flying or floating in the air before his next step."

"You both are exactly correct, and very observant," said the coach.

With each stride, he appears to be in the air just a bit longer. That added airtime shaves fractions of a second off his time and fractions of a second is often the only difference between winning a race and losing a race you should have won.

"Learning to really pump your arms like that will not only make you run faster but will expand your lungs to take in more oxygen to help you run longer with less fatigue," said the coach.

"Harry, it will also help you in your base running for your baseball games. It is important when playing baseball, where the most important step when stealing bases is the first one. Most times a player is safe or thrown out based on the very first step. It is almost more of a timing thing than speed. Practicing that will make you a better base runner and a better ball player. Base running is the difference between a run and an out."

Both boys promised to work on those recommendations from coach H.

CHAPTER 6

"I am sorry but that is all the time we have today, Le Roy, thanks for bringing them in. Those are two very fine young men and I hope I get to see you again real soon," he said.

As the boys were leaving, they asked me how I knew coach H and I said, "Oh never mind."

Coach H overheard the question and called for us to stop.

He said, "You mean your grandfather never told you how we know each other?"

"No sir," the boys replied.

I said, "Patrick, there is no reason to bring up the ancient past and fill their heads with a bunch of nonsense."

"If anything is nonsense it is your last statement. You see boys, quite a few years ago when your grandfather was a Master Chief in the Navy, and I was a young officer just out of Officer Candidate school we were both members of the cruiser USS California's Rescue and Assistance Detail, (R&A detail). We were called upon to provide rescue and assistance to a Spanish transport ship in the Indian Ocean. They had transmitted a S.O.S, (emergency message), that they had an oil fire in their engine room, had evacuated the entire crew to the bridge, had lost all power, and had lost the the ability to steer the ship.

There is a law of the sea that no matter the country a ship is from if you can come to the rescue, you do so, even if the two countries are at war with one another. This law of the sea is above all others. Therefore, our ship loaded up its helicopter with firefighting equipment and half the R&A detail personnel aboard and flew to the rescue of the stricken ship, still a few miles away. While our ship continued to head towards the stricken ship. The plan was to deposit the first half of the R&A detail safely on deck along with the firefighting supplies. Return to our ship and transport the second half of the R&A crew.

The key word was safely. Due to the pitching of the transport ship the helicopter's main rotor blades hit one of the guide wires and that caused the helicopter to crash and slide down the side of the ship. This old grandfather of yours pulled me and then the rest of the R&A detail out of the sinking helicopter. Then while the helicopter was sinking, he went back inside. Cut the pilot and copilot out of their seatbelts and managed to bring them both back to the surface. Ask him to show you the pocketknife he carries with him everywhere, I bet it is the same one.

The rest of the team had found a cargo net and had climbed up the side of the ship. They were waiting on deck as the pilot climbed up the cargo net. Finally, your grandfather helped the copilot, who had injured his arm, navigate the rope cargo net.

When our ship realized what had happened, they sent the second half of the R&A detail and more firefighting equipment over to the ship on the California's motor whale boat. When the second half of the detail joined us, your grandfather asked for volunteers to go down in the engine room with him and put out that roaring inferno. Every man on that detail volunteered to follow your grandfather to put out that fire and they did just that. I believe after the bravery your grandfather displayed that afternoon, the team would have followed him into hell with a bucket of ice water."

"Have him show you the Navy Marine Corps Life Saving Medal

he earned that day for the rescue of me, the other members of the R&A detail, and the pilot, and copilot.

For leading the R&A detail down into the engine room and putting out the fire he was awarded the Bronze Star. Have him show you his other medals too, your grandfather is quite the hero boys. I am running late I really must go."

"Thanks Coach H," the boys chimed in as he left the field house.

"Thanks a lot Patrick," I said. "It will be next to impossible to get the boys to focus on the plans for the rest of the day. All they will want to talk about is medals and what I did in the Navy."

As if on cue, both boys wanted to see the pocketknife I carried with me and wanted to know did I carry it with me all the time, even in church?

CHAPTER 7

Finally, it came to me, one sure fire way to get 10-year-old boys minds off a subject, just mention the word food!

"Who's hungry," I said. I heard nothing but whoops of agreement coming from the back seat. "You just happen to be in luck because I am going to take you to Grandpa's favorite place for hotdogs." It was not really a restaurant, nor was it a food truck, it was a street vendor that had a cart on wheels, and it had a trailer connected to a three-wheel tricycle. I told the boys it was a one-man vendor powered operation.

In a low voice Harry mentioned that the hotdog vendor must not make a very good living selling hotdogs this way. I told them I would fill them in later, when we were in private.

Grandpa must eat here often the boys said, "Because the vendor called him by his first name, Le Roy, and he called the vendor Pete."

I told the boys, "You can call him Mr. Pete."

"Who are these fine young men you have here," Pete asked.

"Just two ragamuffins I found alongside the road," I jokingly replied before telling Pete they were two of my grandsons.

I confirmed to the boys that I was a regular at Mr. Pete's vendor cart when he said, "Two dogs with sauerkraut for you Le Roy as usual, and what are the boys going to have?"

The boys each got a hot dog, one with ketchup and one with mustard. We each grabbed a soda and a bag of chips. There was a park bench in the shade nearby and we ate our hot dogs, not really, I ate mine and the boys inhaled theirs. I glanced their way, and they were each eyeing my second hot dog even though it was loaded with sauerkraut. Unwilling to risk having my arm and shoulder chewed off I asked them if they had room for another. Their faces lit up and their smiles went ear to ear.

They said, "Yes, please."

"Hey, Pete, two more dogs for the boys," I said.

"Coming right up," Pete replied.

Can I read my grandkids or what?

I then told them about Pete. Pete had been a construction supervisor when he had gotten hurt on the job. After a lengthy stay in the hospital, he was told that he could no longer work the long hours he had in the past. That he should investigate a job that he got out in the fresh air and some daily exercise. The hotdog cart was his solution. He has earned enough from working that hotdog cart to put two of his kids through college and paid off the mortgage on their house.

I asked what they thought of Coach H and Harry spoke up and asked Shane if he remembered how many trophies were behind Coach H's desk? Shane said he remembered there were trophies but not how many.

"You both are learning a new skill; I am proud of you."

CHAPTER 8

As soon as lunch was devoured, the boys asked, ""What can we do next?" Then they said, "We want to see all your medals and your pocketknife."

Once again, I shifted the discussion away by saying we can do that any evening. "I thought while we were this close, we could go to the library, there is something I have been wanting to research."

"The library? That is just like being back in school," Harry said.

Shane chimed in with, "We are on summer vacation and that means NO school and NO library."

"You do know that NO adventure can really begin without some clues. That was the first step in finding the Confederate submarine," I said.

Just mentioning the Confederate submarine their brother and sister had helped find two years before had grabbed their immediate attention.

"Are we going to find another lost sunken submarine like the Hunley?"

"No, "I said while chuckling.

"Why not?" they asked in unison.

"Probably because there was not a second Confederate submarine to find, "I replied.

The Hunley was the first and last of its kind during the civil war.

"Why was it so hard to find?" Shane wanted to know. Didn't anyone remember where it was when it was sunk?

"The submarine sank three different times, once next to the pier and five men lost their lives, and twice with all nine crewmen aboard. Only the ghosts of those men knew where she lay on the bottom of the harbor the last time she sank, and they weren't telling anyone."

"What are we going to find clues about at the library today?" they wanted to know.

"I am looking for clues about the underground railroad," I replied.

"I know all about the subway, I've ridden it lots of times when my family goes to Chicago to watch the Chicago Cubs play baseball," Harry explained.

"This is not that kind of underground railroad," I responded. "This kind of railroad was a railroad to freedom." I asked them what they learned about slavery in school or from their parents, and in return I got two deer in the headlights looks. "Let us sit in the cool shade on this park bench outside the library and I will tell you about slavery and maybe a few other things you should know."

"Let me start out by telling you we have a GREAT country; I think the best in the whole world. Our government is a Republic and has lasted over 200 years. It is the longest lasting government in the world. As good as it is, it is far from perfect. If man has his fingers into it, nothing is perfect. There have been some growing pains, and we still have more to go."

Our country has made a ton of mistakes and one of those biggest mistakes was slavery. Slavery in our country started before we were a country. When we were just thirteen colonies owing our allegiance to the King of England, slaves were brought to America."

"When countries like Great Britain made colonies, it was at a great expense and the expectations were that the riches the colonies returned would far exceed their initial investments and thus those countries who started the colonies would profit."

"Some colonies, especially those from Spain searched for gold. Other countries like Great Britain were quick to realize that their thirteen colonies in the new world could supply the mother country with almost unlimited materials. In the northern colonies they got fish, whale oil, furs, and trees to be used as masts for their ships just to mention a few."

"The southern colonies like Virginia, North and South Carolina, and Georgia were much better suited to agriculture. The major crops Great Britain was most interested in were cotton and tobacco. Keep in mind there were no tractors or combines to do all this hard work. Agriculture was very labor intensive and meant spending a lot of time outdoors in sweltering heat. Very few men wanted to work in the fields like that, so the best way was to find someone else to do the hard labor part. Of course, it was much more profitable to have slaves perform these hard jobs because they received no pay. They built little more than shacks for them to live in, fed them a very meager diet, and because they were considered property you could do whatever you wanted with them."

Most people don't understand that slavery started in Africa. In Africa, strong tribes conquered weaker tribes and sold the conquered people to slave traders who packed them in ships so tight it was like a can of sardines.

The slaves were brought to the colonies, mostly in the South where the need was greatest, and they were sold, just like cattle. Families were broken up and ended up not knowing where their children or parents might have ended up. Since they were slaves, they were never paid. They lived in horrible conditions, and often worked to death. They were considered property.

CHAPTER 9

In 1774 our country fought a revolutionary war with Great Britain. The war lasted about seven years. We finally won our independence from Great Britain, the most powerful country of the world at that time. At the beginning of the fight for freedom the Declaration of Independence was written. An initial draft that was supported by the Northern colonies freed all the slaves in all the colonies. It was an easy position for the northern colonies to take because they did not require much slave labor to continue business as usual. Taking slave labor away from the South would have crippled them. The Southern colonies refused to sign the Declaration of Independence and since it would have been impossible for the 13 colonies to fight for their freedom against powerful Great Britain as individual colonies, this forced them to compromise. Independence from Great Britain was the major and immediate concern. The passage freeing the slaves was stricken from the document. The issue of slavery in the United States had been kicked down the road to be dealt with later.

  Had the founding fathers had a crystal ball that could see in the future one hundred years later, perhaps they might have made a different choice. The freedom for slaves' issue would be the cause of our civil war. It caused brother to fight brother and at least 620,000 soldiers along with an untold number of civilian fatalities from both sides died during the American Civil War.

What about the underground railroad they wanted to know.

Life as a slave was barely living. Many slaves were beaten, sold numerous times, and treated no better than farm animals.

Due to living conditions being so bad, punishments so severe, and every man's desire to be free, many slaves took a chance and ran away from the plantations and their owners.

Punishment for running away if they were caught was often death. Not every person in the south believed in slavery. Those that felt that slaves should be free were often referred to as abolitionists. Escaping from the plantation was not easy and even with the help of the abolitionists and people who were sympathetic to the slavery cause, many were captured. Some runaways that were captured only made it to the nearest cottonwood tree and hung. Still others were brought back to the plantation, whipped to within an inch of their life and made an example to others what would happen to them if they were caught running away.

Those that did escape were helped along the way by people who believed slavery was wrong but could not say so in public for fear of being attacked for their beliefs. These people hid slaves in their barns or in secret rooms in their houses. Some even hid them in plain sight pretending they were their slaves doing some farming work for them until the next safe house was available to move them. The people that helped the slaves escape were also in danger should they be caught. Assisting slaves to get from one safe station to the next was kind of like what the railroad does. These stations became known as the <u>"Underground Railroad"</u>.

Some of the people who took the most risk in moving slaves along the underground railroad were themselves escaped slaves.

The most famous was a woman named Harriet Tubman. She was a true American hero and a visionary. She was born into slavery, in Dorchester County, Maryland. She was beaten and whipped by her various masters as a child. Early in life, she suffered a bad head wound when an irate overseer threw a heavy metal weight intending to hit another slave but hit her instead. The injury caused dizziness, pain, and caused her to have great difficulty sleeping, throughout the rest of her life. After her injury, Tubman began experiencing strange visions and vivid dreams, which she believed were messages sent from God. These experiences, combined with her Methodist upbringing, led her to become devoutly religious.

In 1849, she escaped to Philadelphia, only to return to Maryland to rescue her family soon after. Slowly, one group at a time, she brought relatives with her out of the state, and eventually guided dozens of other slaves to freedom. Traveling by night and in extreme secrecy, Tubman (or "Moses," as she was called) "never lost a passenger". Before long, just getting a slave across the line into a free state was not enough. Slave hunters would pursue them. If they were caught, they would be placed in chains and taken back to the plantation they had escaped from. This practice required Harriet to escort the newly freed slaves to travel even further north into Canada to become free.

That is not her only claim to fame. When the Civil War began, she worked for the Union Army, first as a cook and nurse, and then as an armed scout and spy. She became the first woman to lead an armed expedition in the war, she guided the raid at Combahee Ferry, which liberated more than 700 slaves. In her later years, she was an activist in the movement for women's right to vote.

She became an icon of courage and freedom.[1]

It became logical to use railroad terms for this transfer of people. People that helped the slaves move were called conductors, the slaves were referred to as passengers, and destinations were called stations. Using this secret code allowed those connected to the movement of the passengers to speak out in the open with no one aware.

My grandsons were now "onboard" with going to the library so let the adventure begin.

Following a short venture to the library it was back home for some pool time. The boys wanted to see my medals, and especially my pocketknife. I could tell they needed to burn off some of that energy before doing anything else.

They ran, and jumped, and splashed in the pool for a few hours before supper. They were so tired they almost fell asleep right in their mashed potatoes.

CHAPTER 10

The next morning, they both ate a full breakfast and were ready to start the days adventure. Both boys looked sad when I explained that today was a workday.

"A workday," they said in unison.

"You saw my big garden out there. Did you think it picked itself? Where did you think those carrots came from that you had with supper last night? I know you both enjoyed the strawberry shortcake Grandma made last night. You each had two helpings. It probably wouldn't have tasted so good without the strawberries."

"This morning while it is still cool, we are going to harvest some of our berries, tomatoes, cucumbers, and onions. "

Shane said, "but I don't like onions."

"That is okay" I said, "you sure did not mind the flavoring they gave the roast and gravy last night at dinner."

Both boys shook their heads up and down followed by a yes, Grandpa.

We collected the berry baskets and out to the garden we went. We picked strawberries, raspberries, and blueberries. When we had enough, we took them back to the house. Grandma Judy chose a few baskets and took them into the kitchen but there were a lot left.

"What is Grandma Judy going to do with those berries?" Shane wanted to know.

"Well, I know she was going to make strawberry and raspberry jam. It will not surprise me a bit to find blueberry muffins to go with supper tonight and probably show up in your pancakes tomorrow morning," I answered.

"What are we going to do with all of the rest of the stuff we picked?" Harry asked.

After lunch I will show you.

During lunch Shane commented that he really liked the bread that his turkey sandwich was on. "What kind of bread is it?"

Again, I laughed. "That is Grandma bread," I replied.

"What is Grandma bread?" they both wanted to know.

It is bread that your grandmother makes, I laughed.

"Don't they sell bread in the store here in Alabama?" Shane asked.

"Of course, they do, but they do not sell that kind of bread in any store, because your grandmother adds a special ingredient into everything she makes." The boys were all ears ready to hear a BIG family secret. "She adds love into everything she makes." The boys just smiled.

CHAPTER 11

After lunch we loaded the remaining berry baskets into the back of the truck and went out to deliver the remaining berries. We stopped at certain houses, the boys left the truck, grabbed a couple of berry baskets, left them on the porch, rang the bell, and then ran back to the truck. Most people waved at us. Some who got to the door fast enough said thank you to the boys.

"Grandpa why do you have a garden and why do you grow so much stuff if you give most of it away?"

"That is a question that has many answers." I smiled. "First, I enjoy my garden. I like the different varieties I can grow. If you are limiting yourself to what the grocery store is selling you are very limited indeed."

"For instance, this year I grew four different varieties of carrots. I grew baby carrots that Grandma likes to have in her salad. I grew carrots that ripen early and only get to be 6" long. I grew some early carrots that are ready to eat in the first part of July. And finally, I grew carrots that are extra hardy and long that will go in our root cellar and last us through the winter.

"Another thing is freshness." I continued "Take strawberries, the ones you buy in the store might be three weeks old before they show up on the grocer's shelf."

"Why aren't they spoiled?" Harry asked.

"That is because they are not ripe when they are picked in the farmers field. They ripen while they are being shipped. Many fruits and vegetables start losing their flavor and vitamins as soon as they are picked. So, instead of eating strawberries that were harvested three weeks ago in California. I prefer my own strawberries. Which do you think will taste better? Believe me our berries taste so much better after they have ripened on the vine instead of a box on the truck.

"Secondly, I like being able to give fresh vegetables to friends, neighbors, and those less fortunate. It is my way of giving back to someone else. Although, the number one reason is my fruits and vegetables just taste better. "

"Why did we give all those berries away?" they wanted to know.

"Everyone you gave berries to today has one kind of challenge or another. Some have been ill or lost a family member. Others are older and cannot do gardening anymore. Some people, through no fault of their own, just cannot afford buying them in the grocery store."

"Why don't they just plant their own garden the way you did?" the boys asked.

"Growing a garden takes a lot of time, many of the people work a full-time job and then must prepare dinner, review children's homework, do laundry, clean the house, you get the idea. Being a parent is a huge responsibility and it takes a lot of time to maintain a house and raise kids right. I did not have time to garden until I retired either."

I enjoy giving, it just makes me feel good, and it is the right thing to do.

Just before we started down the driveway, I reached into one of the pockets of my overalls and brought out two identical small boxes. The boys tore open the brown paper wrapping and each one was looking at a pocketknife, like mine only a smaller version.

"For us?" they asked.

"Yes, for you, but there are some rules you must agree to before you can have them. Both boys nodded in agreement. While you are here under my care you may carry them with you. When your mom and dad come back to pick you up you must surrender them to your parents. Your parents will decide when and if you are allowed to carry them. If they choose to take them away for a certain period, I don't want to hear that you gave them any back talk is that clear? You may NEVER, NEVER ever take them to school."

"Times have changed since when I went to school, the rules have gotten a lot tougher. Should you get caught with them in school you will more than likely be turned over to the police, expelled from school for the rest of that school year, and have a criminal record that will follow you the rest of your lives. A knife is a tool and should only be used as a tool. If you have friends come over to your house, you are not to show them the knife or even tell them about it. Do I make myself perfectly clear?"

Both boys agreed.

As they marveled at having their own knives, they once again asked, "where are we going now Grandpa?"

"We have two more boxes to deliver to a friend of mine."

We pulled in the drive and two Labrador Retrievers sounded the alarm and met us at the truck.

"Boy's," I said, "Meet Duke and Duchess." The boys were almost as excited as the Labs.

I tooted on the horn and Dr. Lee came out. I introduced the boys and told them to get the remaining boxes of vegetables and berries out of the truck and we followed Dr. Lee into the house.

Both Duke and Duchess were VERY interested in the contents of the boxes the boys were carrying.

CHAPTER 12

Dr. Lee told us how old the house was and how they were breathing new life into the house one room at a time. She and her family had only bought the house a week ago. She gave us a tour of the downstairs and then when our backs were turned, she just disappeared. There was no other way out of the room, yet she was gone. Suddenly a panel in the wall moved and a secret room appeared where there was no room before and there was Dr. Lee.

"So, what do you think of our little hidden room?" she asked. "We contacted the local historical society and they confirmed there was evidence that there was a very active underground railway station in town, but they had no idea where all the stations were located."

"Dr. Lee, may we go inside and look around?" the boys asked.

"Sure, let me get a couple of flashlights first," she said.

She handed them both a flashlight and the boys hurried inside. The room was a lot bigger than they had imagined. When they shined their flashlight beams on the floor, they noticed that one section of the flooring was different than the rest. It looked like it was made of a different kind of wood and didn't look as old.

They each withdrew the pocket knife their grandfather had given them the and began to dig around the odd-looking panel. By working together, they lifted it out and looked down the hole underneath.

They could see the ground. Harry dropped through and Shane handed him the panel and together, they followed the path that took them under the front porch. The entrance to the path was guarded by two hedges. Harry and Shane walked back in the house and snuck up on Dr. Lee and me. "How did you boys get out of that hidden room without us seeing you?" I asked. Harry explained the panel in the floor entrance they had found that allowed them to leave the hidden room.

"Unfortunately, that same exit you found from the hidden room would allow someone to sneak in the house unannounced," I said.

I had the boys show me the way they had come and we reentered the secret room from underneath the house in what is called a crawl space. Soon we were back in the living room with Dr. Lee.

Dr. Lee said, "that must have been the way slaves entered and left the hidden room 150 years ago to prevent being seen. It probably hasn't been opened since the end of the civil war."

Shane handed me the panel they had removed, and I looked it over very carefully. On the bottom of the panel there was a handle screwed into the panel. "Doctor, the problem with what you just said was that this panel was used a lot later than 150 years ago."

"How do you know?" Dr. Lee asked.

For one thing the screws that were used to attach this handle aren't that old and more telling is the manufacturing seal on the handle says, "Made in China 2022".

Dr. Lee said, "So someone may have been living in this house before we bought it. I'm sure as soon as we moved in whomever was using it is long gone."

I told her "Just to make sure, I should get my hammer out of the toolbox in my truck and the boys, and I will seal it up for you just to be sure. You never know what kind of critters may have been coming and going. Raccoons are a darn nuisance and can make a mess in your house in just a short period of time.'

Dr. Lee said, "not to bother, her husband would be home in

three days, and she would have him do it. She wanted to show him what the boys had found."

I told Dr. Lee that if she changed her mind, I would be happy to put a few nails in the trap door and secure it until her husband got home. "Feel free to give me a call should you need anything until your husband gets back," I promised.

She said, "I'm sure I will be fine, I have the Duke and Duchess to protect me. I'm sure I won't need to call you, but thanks for the offer."

I said, "If you change your mind, just give me a call."

The boys asked if they could continue exploring the room because they really hadn't looked it over very closely once they had spied the trap door. I handed them the piece of flooring they had removed and told them to put it back like they found it.

Dr. Lee said, "Go right ahead, then she said Boys will be Boys."

This time we followed the boys in the secret room and watched as the boys played their light beams on every inch of the room from floor to ceiling. Because the secret room was partly built under the staircase there were a whole bunch of nail points sticking down. They glistened in the light like the teeth of a great white shark.

Harry spotted something stuck in the far corner under the stairs. You could just see a dark color that didn't match the rest. Dr. Lee had said they had cleaned out the entire room she couldn't believe they had missed something.

"Do you think you can reach it?" Shane asked.

"I think so," Harry said. "I just don't want to get stuck on any of those nails." By lying on his stomach and reaching as far as he could, he snagged it and pulled it along the floor.

Dr. Lee said, "no telling what kind of germs are on the points of those old nails. If you get so much as a small scratch, you will have to get a tetanus shot."

Harry slid across his belly on the floor until Shane told him it was safe to stand up. In his hand he held a thin book.

Harry handed the book they had found to Dr. Lee who carefully opened the book and took a deep breath.

"Do you boys know what you found?" she asked.

Both boys shook their heads. This appears to be a ledger listing all the slaves who passed through this station. It lists the dates, their ages, and when they arrived and left for the next station. This is an amazing piece of history you boys have uncovered, and positively proves that this house was part of the underground railroad. She turned some pages and let out a happy squeal.

I looked over her shoulder as she paged through the book and quickly realized this station was active way before the civil war. The people who owned this house were abolitionists. If the totals on the bottom of each page were to be believed there were hundreds, if not thousands, of slaves that passed through this station on their way to freedom. There was a separate column for men, women, and children. It also listed their destination they wanted to go and, in some cases, where they came from.

Dr. Lee wanted to know why they would keep such a dangerous document and why they kept it in with the slaves.

I told her that keeping the ledger was kind of like a get out of jail free card. The people living there at the time must have heard about Sherman's march to the sea. He was burning just about anything of value that his troops encountered. If his troops happened upon this grand house, being able to show that ledger and the number of slaves that had passed through this house on the way to freedom may have saved it from being torched with almost every other house in town. Sherman used the term "Total War" in his drive to the sea. He destroyed anything and everything the Confederate's could use to extend the war. That included these big old estate homes like hers.

Keeping it in the slave's hidden room was probably the safest place to keep it. If the room was discovered, the jig was up, ledger or no ledger.

We left the dark hidden room and Dr. Lee clung to that ledger as if it were gold.

She took it to her desk in the corner and with a calculator added the totals from each page.

She said, "it says here that almost two thousand slaves passed through this station on their way to freedom. I can't wait to take this to the historical society. I'm sure once they have examined it, they will verify it is authentic and then display it in their museum. Our house will even get a historical marker."

"We are treasure hunters just like in the movie "Raiders of the Lost Ark," Shane said.

Everyone started laughing.

Dr. Lee looked at her watch and said," I hate to end this gathering of young treasure hunters, but unfortunately I have another call for work I have to take."

She thanked us again for the berries and especially finding the ledger, and then handed Grandpa three dozen eggs.

CHAPTER 13

Everyone climbed back in the truck and headed back home.

Where did she get the eggs, the boys wanted to know.

"Where do eggs come from?" I asked the boys. They both chimed in with chickens. "That's right. In her spare time Dr. Lee raises chickens. Every time I deliver berries or other things from my garden, she gives me 3 dozen eggs. No one sets the price for the eggs or the fruits and vegetables it is just one friend helping another. Your grandmother will make lots of good things with these eggs. You will probably see some of them for breakfast tomorrow."

We drove home. The boys couldn't wait to go treasure hunting someplace else. After supper we gathered around the fire pit, and I told them what it was like for me and their grandmother growing up. They couldn't believe that we had known each other all our lives. They laughed when I told them how I used to tease her with garter snakes I found and how she would scream and run home.

"You did that to Grandma Judy, and she still married you?"

Yup, that is amazing. "She has stuck with me for 40 years."

"You sure must have used some powerful super glue to have her stick with you for that long," Harry replied.

We all had a good chuckle after that.

After a much-needed shower, it was bedtime. Dreams of adventures to come danced in their heads.

Judy and I continued to sit by the fire pit and watch the red embers slowly turn to gray.

Abby the wonder dog laying between us allowing us to take turns petting her.

You know Judy said, "They have not asked once for their video games their parents left for them."

"I know," I said. "I'm the one who hid them and for the life of me I probably won't remember where I hid them until their parents come back to pick them up."

Judy said, "I haven't heard your television come on either, not even for your baseball games."

"Who needs baseball games when you have two 10-year-old grandsons who like adventures just as much as I do?"

CHAPTER 14

At breakfast the next day we had scrambled eggs, and the topic came up that the county fair was coming up next month and there would probably be lots of rides, games, and fun things to eat.

"Can we go to the county fair?" Shane asked.

"Don't worry about missing the fair, your grandfather hasn't missed one since he got out of the Navy and returned home. Besides he wouldn't miss a chance to show off his fruits and vegetables."

"What are we going to do today?" Harry asked.

"Today I thought you boys would pick berries this morning and sell them this afternoon, you could make some money to go on those rides, play games, and have some of those fun things to eat at the county fair. Would you like that?" I asked.

Both boys hit the back door running to get the berry baskets and start their very own berry business.

Judy said, "Le Roy you should be ashamed of yourself, you know perfectly well their parents left money with us to entertain the boys while they were here."

"Better to let them learn a little bit about business and how money doesn't grow on trees," I said.

While the boys were occupied for the next few hours, I built them a stand from some spare boards I had lying around. I made some **Berries for Sale** signs and posted them up and down the road.

By then the boys had completed the berry picking. I told them to go for a quick dip before their grandmother had lunch ready for them.

Lunch was toasted cheese sandwiches, a bowl of tomato soup, and some funny shaped pickles.

In a matter of moments, the toasted cheese sandwiches and tomato soup had disappeared, leaving only the funny shaped pickles.

The boys turned up their noses at the funny shaped pickles.

I told them that you will never know if you are going to like something unless you try it. Hesitantly, each boy picked up a pickle slice and took a tiny bite. They had been so sure they weren't going to like the pickles. The shock that came over their faces was priceless. They quickly downed those pickles and were asking for more.

"What kind of pickles were they? Where did you buy them? Can we get some to take home with us when we must leave?" They peppered their grandmother with questions.

Grandma said, "They are called Icicle Pickles. You can't buy them in a store. I made them from a recipe my mother gave to me."

"Why is your food so much better here than what my mom makes?" Shane asked. "Mom makes us tomato soup, but it doesn't taste as good as your tomato soup."

"That's because my tomato soup comes from tomatoes picked fresh from Grandpa's Garden and Your mom gets it from a can. You need to understand your mom is teaching school, taking care of most of the household chores, and taking you every-where you need to go. I have the time to prepare meals that your mom just doesn't have. When you guys are grown and out of the house and she becomes a grandma she will have the time."

"Just great," Harry said, with a smile on his face. "Our moms won't learn how to cook until we are in college."

Everyone laughed.

The boys got out to their stand and were only there about 15 minutes when their first customer pulled in. I watched as the boys made change. Sometimes they had to use the pencil and paper to get it right, but all the customers were very patient with the junior salesmen. The boys wanted to use a calculator, but I told them I didn't own one. Nothing wrong with a little white lie when teaching grandchildren.

In a little over an hour, they were sold out. Most of the customers asking if they would be there tomorrow. I told them, weather permitting, the day after they would be back with more fresh fruit and vegetables.

CHAPTER 15

The boys took their money box to the kitchen and started to count their money. They had made $78.00 in a little over an hour.

The boys wanted to know why people aren't selling fruits and vegetables like they are.

I explained that was probably because you two are only seeing one side of what is called the supply chain. If you have the land to put in a garden to raise your own fruits and vegetables, you still have costs. You must buy the plants or seeds, hire someone to till your garden with a plow, buy fertilizer, weed the garden. Let's not forget the cost of finding a way to keep the birds out of them and the bugs. All that cut into any profit you might make at the stand. Then you have the labor portion of the equation. How much is your time worth, while you are planting, watering, weeding, and selling at the fruit and vegetable stand? When you add up all the costs you will be lucky if you are making $1.00 an hour. For most people the money they make from a full-time job far exceeds the money they would make selling fruits and vegetables from a roadside stand. I don't do it for profit, I do it because I enjoy it. Because of that I ignore the costs.

They wanted to know if their brother Jack and sister Bianca had done the same thing two years ago when they spent the summer with us. They started out selling berries just like you did but after they were comfortable selling berries, they started selling tomatoes, zucchini squash, carrots, and new potatoes.

"We can do that too," they exclaimed.

"That will mean you will have to put in a lot more garden time and less pool and play time too. They said that they didn't care. They wanted to top what their brother and sister did two years ago. (Competition is such a good motivation tool.)

There was still time, so I took them down to see Miss Carol who works at the bank. We set up a bank account for Shane and Harry enterprises and deposited $70.00.

Miss Carol wanted to hear all about our berry sales and asked when we would be open again because she wanted to get some berries too. The boys took the receipt and the remaining $8.00 and went out to the parking lot.

Both boys wanted to know why they hadn't deposited the other $8.00. I told them they had earned a reward and now they had enough to buy some ice cream cones. Their faces lit up like the night sky during a fourth of July fireworks display.

"I think the ice cream tastes just a bit better when you can take pride in the fact that you had earned it instead of it just being given to you," I said. The boys were too busy licking their ice cream cones to respond.

Their grandmother had not been idle while we were gone. She had baked potatoes, pork chops, gravy, blue berry muffins, and something new called green bean casserole. For dessert she had made my very favorite jelly roll.

Boys, do you realize that everything we had for supper comes from our own garden, except the pork chops?

They were too busy chowing down to answer. We had two boys with healthy appetites. There wasn't a scrap of food left on those plates for poor old Abby.

CHAPTER 16

Sooner or later, I knew it was going to happen. It rained, and the weatherman said, "expect the rain to last all day."

When I asked them what they wanted to do, they unanimously said they wanted to see my medals. and your pocketknife.

I told them I didn't remember where I had put the medals. Wouldn't you know it, they asked their grandmother if she knew where they were, and of course she knew exactly where that stuff was.

I gave her "the look".

She said, "Don't you dare give me that look. You should be proud of the medals you earned. Let the boys think of you as the hero you are and have always been. Boys need to have someone to look up to."

———

Their grandmother brought down an old ammo can that I thought I had hidden in the closet.

Boy, that woman doesn't miss much.

They opened the metal box and looked inside. "Wow! Shane exclaimed; you have a lot of medals."

They lay the medals all out in a row and fired so many questions at me so fast I didn't know which one to answer first. Luckily their grandmother came to the rescue. She turned on the computer, connected to the internet and told the boys to look up each one of the medals. She told them, *write down the name, write down what it is, and then when you have done that for all the medals, your grandfather will tell you how he earned each one, where he was when he earned it, and how old he was. I will listen in and make sure he doesn't leave out any details.*

Both boys raced to the computer to complete the task their grandmother had given them. It took them the better part of an hour to complete their search and return with the list. They called out each medal by name and then I would retrieve the medal from the line the boys had put them in. They would look it over as if they expected it to grow legs and crawl away.

Most of them are just, "I was there medals," I said.

The boys looked confused.

"It just means the ship was in a certain place at a certain time We did the job we were assigned to do, and we got the award. Like that blue and yellow one that is the Navy Expeditionary medal, which was awarded to the entire ship during the Iranian Hostage Crisis."

"What was the Iranian Hostage crisis?" they wanted to know.

"In most countries we are friends with and even some we are not friends with we have established something called an embassy."

"An embassy is the residence of our government officials in a foreign country who represent our country. Many large governments, like the United States, United Kingdom, and other European countries, have embassies located all over the world where they provide services to members of their home country abroad. They help travelers should they lose their passports or have need of other services. Embassies also work with local governments and organizations on shared interests. The land that the embassy sits on, although in a foreign country, is supposed to be as if it belonged to the country who has their diplomats working there. Although each embassy has a small group of military personnel assigned, they are just to provide basic security until the host country can respond to any major crisis."

"What became known as the Iran hostage crisis began on November 4, 1979, when a group of Iranian students in Tehran, the capital of Iran, stormed the American embassy. The small Marine detachment that was supposed to hold out until Iran sent in the military to put down the protest finally got overrun. Iran never sent its military. This failure to act trapped fifty-two American workers there and held them hostage for 444 days (about 1 year 2 and a half months)."[1]

"Were you one of the hostages? Harry wanted to know."

"I shook my head no. However, I was a hostage in another way. I was assigned to the nuclear cruiser USS California, and it became our job to sit just off the coast in international waters. We were to provide an early warning to our aircraft carrier that was stationed further out to sea where it was safer."

"What was your job on the cruiser Grandpa?" Shane asked.

"I oversaw number two engine room, I had about 35 men that worked for me. We operated and maintained one of the two ships nuclear reactors. The reactors heat water which provides steam that turns turbines to make electricity and provide propulsion. We also took sea water and made fresh water for the entire ship.

"We weren't out there 444 days, but we were out there almost a year."

As I remembered, I started laughing. The boys wanted to know what was so funny.

"Of the year we were there I think they served us roast beef for 200 days."

I told them that because we were a nuclear ship, we didn't have to refuel every three or four days. Our Nuclear ship didn't have to refuel for twenty-five years.

CHAPTER 17

I told them what limited our ship to how long we could be gone was food. When a ship goes to sea it starts out with fresh fruits, vegetables, and milk. After about 10 days (about 1 and a half weeks) the vegetables are shot. Fruits and milk last about 15 days. After that it is canned fruits and powdered milk. The canned fruits and vegetables are okay. The powdered milk takes some getting used to. The one meat that lasts the longest is roast beef. We once had roast beef for 87 straight days. There are just so many ways you can fix roast beef. I didn't think that I could ever look at another roast beef or even a cow for that matter.

Grandma chimed in, "well it seems to me after watching you eat dinner the other night, you and roast beef are once again on speaking terms." We all laughed.

The boys insisted I had to tell them about each medal. Thanks to Coach Hilgendorf they seemed very interested in the details about the bronze star and the Navy Marine Corps lifesaving medal.

They seemed especially interested in the surface warfare pin, what it meant, and what I had to do to earn it.

I explained it meant you had to be more than just an expert in your job, you had to learn how the rest of the ship worked. I learned how to wash clothes in the ship's laundry, to drop the ships anchor, how to use signal flags, and even how to load and fire torpedoes.

The boys seemed mystified. I think that minute if I had been a Navy Recruiter and the boys both 18 instead of 10 they would have joined the Navy.

We spent the rest of the afternoon with me telling sea stories and them hanging on every word. I told them how we made fresh water out of salt water. Explained how we used the ships nuclear reactors to make steam that then went to the turbines that drove the ship through the water and to make our own electricity. I don't think I have ever had anyone hang on every word like these boys did.

CHAPTER 18

It had finally stopped raining and I decided to teach the boys how to catch their own fishing worms called night crawlers.

After the rain these long worms come to the surface and stretch out most of the way from their holes. They keep a portion inside to help with a rapid escape should they feel threatened. If anything scares them, they go back in the hole in an instant.

The boys wanted to know why do the worms come out of the ground after it rains? Wouldn't it be safer if they just stayed underground?

Scientists still haven't figured that out yet, but they have three thoughts.

- Worms don't have lungs. They breathe through their skin. They need moisture-enriched soil with a certain oxygen content to survive.

Very wet soil won't necessarily drown a worm because they can live fully submerged for days if oxygen levels are right. However, according to Penn State University, worms can suffocate in soaked soil if conditions are wrong. So, they move to the surface to avoid that.

- To get around faster

Many scientists agree that worms tend to use soaked soil days as migration days. They can't travel as fast while burrowing tunnels under the ground, and it's too dry above ground on rain-free days for them to survive.

So, a soaking rain allows them to slither to the surface and move gracefully on the wet ground.

- To get away from a predator that might or might not be there.

Some scientists believe the sound of the rain hitting the ground makes worms think they're in danger of moles. So, they make a beeline towards the surface as a way of escape.[1]

I demonstrated that even though the worms have no eyes they can sense the light and poof, they are gone back in the ground. You use the flashlight, but you don't shine it directly on them.

I laughed as at first more worms got away than got caught. Pretty soon they got the hang of it and in about 30 minutes they had caught plenty for the next day's activities.

"I told them before we call it a night, I need to set a trap for crickets." The boys looked at me like I was from Mars when I told them to grab one of their grandmother's freshly baked loaves of bread."

"You may not want to let her catch you taking one." Better to make her wonder how it disappeared.

With loaf of bread in hand, I took out my pocketknife cut one end off and handed it to the boys who promptly made that evidence disappear.

I demonstrated the proper technique to scoop out most of the inside of the loaf leaving what looked like a bread cave. I then set it in the long grass overnight.

CHAPTER 19

The boys were up almost as soon as the sun was this morning. The first thing they wanted to see was if our cricket trap had caught any crickets. We checked the cricket trap, and it was full of crickets. We placed the whole loaf of bread in the box I had made for holding crickets. The bread would give them food for several days. If we kept them in the box more than a couple of days we would have to slice up an apple and put it inside. I could tell they wanted to know why they would need an apple. I explained to them the apple would give them something to eat and the moisture from the apple would provide them something to drink.

After breakfast it was time to gather up fruits and vegetables from the garden to sell in their stand today. They decided to sell strawberries, blueberries, raspberries, tomatoes, summer squash, and Grandma's favorite, broccoli. We discussed pricing and I showed them how to wash the vegetables first to make them more presentable to the customers.

In between customers the boys wanted to know if I had run a stand like this when I was their age. That brought back the memories. "Boys, I did run a stand like this but that was not my first sales business. I used to catch and sell night crawlers to the local bait shop. I think I was about 7 years old. Mr. Curtiss, who owned the bait shop, used to pay me a penny apiece for every nightcrawler I brought in. When I first started Mr. Curtiss would ask me how many I had, I would tell him, and then together we would dump them out and count them. After the third time when I came in the shop to deliver my worms, he asked me how many I had. I told him, and he would tell me to just add them to the worm box. He never checked my count ever again. I was not the only boy delivering night crawlers, but I was the only boy that he didn't check the count. Why do you think that was?"

The boys said, "It was because he could trust you not to cheat."

"That's right," I agreed. "It paid off in other little ways too. If I was in the bait shop and Mr. Curtiss had a lot of customers, he would have me go in the back and get the bait the anglers wanted. Almost every time I did, he would give me a quarter. He called it a tip. That first year I think I made a little over one hundred dollars to put in my savings account just from selling the earth worms and the tips."

You mean you had a savings account just like us? Shane said.

"That's right, my grandfather took me to the same bank we went to today and opened an account. My first deposit was only $5.00."

"Did Miss Carol help you open your account like she did us?"

"Just how old do you think Miss Carol is?" I said laughingly.

I couldn't wait to tell Carol next time I saw her in church.

That day's fruit and vegetable sale went even better than their first day. They counted out their money and couldn't wait to deposit the days take in their savings account.

I told them we would go to the bank tomorrow on our way to our next adventure. "What is it?" they both asked.

"Tomorrow, we go digging for diamonds," I said. You should have seen the way their eyes lit up.

"You mean you know where to find diamonds," they asked. I just nodded my head yes. That night while they were sleeping, I am sure visions of diamonds danced in their heads.

CHAPTER 20

After another hearty breakfast of biscuits and sausage gravy. We stopped in the tool shed and chose some shovels, hammers, and a twist drill that we added to the bed of the truck. Their Grandmother brought out a jug of lemonade and sandwiches she had lovingly packed for today's adventure.

First stop the bank. We entered the bank and Miss Carol greeted us and wanted to know what she could do to help. The boys handed her what they had made at the fruit and vegetable stand for the past two days.

"How much is in here?" she asked. as they handed her the bag. She began to count it out at the teller window.

The boys proudly said, "$125.00."

"Wow! You boys are doing great with your savings. Are you saving up for something special?"

"We are saving up for the county fair next month they both replied in unison."

"Good for you, you are off to a great start, Miss Carol smiled. Learning to save and working towards a goal are great things to learn early. Do you know how a bank works?"

The boys shook their heads no.

Miss Carol told them that when you put money into the bank as savings, the bank can then loan it out to someone who needs it, maybe to buy a new car, or put a new roof on their house.

"You mean our money could be in some guy's car going down the road? What if we want our money back? You said we could take it out anytime we wanted. How can we do that if it is in some guy's new car?"

Carol and I just chuckled.

"The bank keeps some money in reserve, she continued. What is really happening is that some of the bank's reserve money is driving down the road in that new car. Your money and the money of other bank customers money replaces some of the reserve. For letting the bank use your money the bank pays you a little bit of interest depending on how much you are lending the bank and how long you keep it in the bank. The bank also charges interest to the customer who borrowed the money to buy that new car. The interest we charge for borrowing money is more than the interest we pay you. That difference is how the bank makes money."

We left the bank, got back in the truck, and headed off to dig for diamonds.

CHAPTER 21

The boys wanted to know how to find diamonds. I told them it might be harder than you think. The diamonds are usually found in a special kind of rock called Dolostone or vuggy rock. Inside some of the vuggy rocks are cavities. These cavities can be smaller than a pea or several feet across. If you are lucky, inside a cavity, you will find one or more diamonds.

But don't get too excited they aren't really diamonds. They are a mineral called quartz. Like a diamond they are strong enough to scratch glass. We unloaded our tools and went inside the mineral display building, paid our entrance fee, and looked at some of the diamonds on display discovered on the grounds.

"Now that you know what you are looking for, let's go find them," I said. We climbed up and over a rock pile until the boys thought they found some vuggy rocks that they thought looked promising. Before the boys could start their hunt for these hidden diamonds, I handed out work gloves and safety glasses.

The boys lifted their heavy hammers and hit the rock and the hammers bounced off. They were amazed the rock didn't open on the first whack.

"You don't expect mother nature to give up her treasures that easy, do you?" I said.

After a few whacks they managed to break open the vuggy rock but, after a close examination, found there were no diamonds. The boys started taking turns hitting the rocks. Nothing seemed to be the only thing they found the first hour, and then they struck pay dirt. They had been hammering on a big rock and when it cracked open, inside the center of the rock there were several cavities now exposed. They found their first diamonds. They brought them over to me and we examined them closely. Most of them were about the size of one of my garden peas but two of them were a very good size. The mining adventure continued for another two hours until the boys were too worn out to lift their heavy hammers another time.

We gathered up our tools and our diamonds and headed back to the truck. The boys had unearthed about two dozen of the diamonds. They were looking forward to telling their friends back home all about finding diamonds.

I drove the truck down a country lane I knew about. Soon we were parked in the shade of a group of cottonwood trees overlooking a pond. On the way to the cottonwood trees, I had driven past several NO TRESPASSING signs. Posted all along the ponds bank were NO FISHING signs.

I put the tailgate down and we broke out our lunches.

Child Trafficking and the Underground Railroad

Grandpa they said, "We don't think we are supposed to be here." I just acted as if I didn't hear them.

CHAPTER 22

They just shook their heads in disbelief that I would ignore all those signs. After lunch we collected our trash and put it in the waste bag I had brought just for that purpose.

"Now we are going to try and catch some catfish for dinner tonight," I said. "Luckily I brought some fishing poles and nightcrawlers with us."

We had just finished baiting our hooks, we could hear a motor and soon a farmer on an old tractor appeared. He got down off the tractor and the boys thought I was going to get yelled at and kicked off the land. When he got close enough his face had a big smile.

He said, "Le Roy are these your grandsons?"

"They surely are," I replied as we shook hands. I introduced my grandsons to Mr. Will.

Will said, "When we were boys like you, we went to school together, we were both in the cub scouts, and when we turned sixteen, we became junior volunteer firefighters. Then your grandfather ran off and joined the Navy. I stayed back and worked on the family farm. I think we have known each other for over 60 years."

"Boys," I said, 'you were right to question me for coming this way. We should ALWAYS obey no trespassing signs unless you first have permission. After you boys went to bed last night, I called Will and got permission to bring you fishing in his catfish pond. It never hurts to ask permission, and if you are respectful and have a good name in town you just might be granted permission even if it is posted. Most landowners have posted their land because of bad experiences in the past."

With Will's help, the boys soon had their lines in the water and were catching some very hungry catfish. Will hopped back on his tractor and headed back to his farm. As soon as we had six nice eating size catfish, I called a stop. The boys looked at me in disbelief.

"But Grandpa," they said, "the fish are biting really good, and we can probably catch a whole mess."

"I'm sure you could, but how many are you going to eat? How many are you going to clean? How many do you expect your grandmother to cook?" I replied. "We should never take more than we need, that goes for everything in life."

"Are you extra hungry grandpa?" Harry wanted to know.

"Why do you ask?" I said.

"Because there are only four of us and we have six fish." Harry stated.

"We are going to drop two of them at Mr. Will's house for letting us fish in his pond," I said.

"Which ones should we give him?" the boys asked.

"Which two are the biggest?" I asked.

The boys pointed them out. "There is your answer, It probably doesn't matter to Will, but it never hurts to go a bit extra. That is what people remember."

"When I was about your age, I used to mow lawns. When I hired on to mow a lawn, I also edged the sidewalks and the driveway. I also swept the cut grass from the driveway and the sidewalk too. It was the difference in doing the job 75% or doing the job 100%. There were a lot of kids my age looking for lawn mowing jobs all spring, summer, and fall. But who do you think got the job? The kid doing 75% or the one doing 100%?"

The boys both nodded.

We went home and I cleaned the fish while the boys splashed in the pool.

CHAPTER 23

I asked them where tonight's meal had come from. They started off with the catfish Grandma had fried. We had biscuits that Grandma had made, carrots, and parsnips both from our garden and picked this morning. They guessed everything except the milk, butter, and honey we gathered ourselves. "Don't be so quick to rule out the milk," I said. "We get our milk and butter from a farmer down the road, usually trading a couple of apple pies when it comes apple picking time, and some vegetables from my garden."

"The honey came from Mr. & Mrs. Sparks who raise bees in their back yard."

"The point I am trying to teach you boys is that if all you had in your bank account is $50.00, if you can grow your own food. If you have friends who will let you fish in their pond, and if you have established good relations with your neighbors, you can eat close to free. That $50.00 can be used for something else you may need."

"How do you pay for the honey from the Sparks family?" Shane asked. Your grandmother babysits for the two youngest Sparks children during the school year while the parents' work. To make the Sparks family happy, your grandmother accepts $25.00 a week which is way below the rate for babysitting."

"Does grandma have her own bank account?" Shane asked.

"Actually no," I replied. "We don't have separate bank accounts."

"One of the biggest problems many marriages have is about money. Your grandmother and I agreed early on that we didn't want that risk, so all the money became OUR money."

"Your grandmother and I talked it over and since we didn't need the money from her babysitting, we decided that we would anonymously gift it back to the Sparks family just before Christmas. They go out of their way to help their neighbors and have five children they are raising."

"Don't you two go and spoil things by telling them," I warned.

Both boys assured me their lips were sealed.

"Help your grandmother with the dishes, take out the garbage, and I will feed and water Abby. If everyone pitches in, I might be able to squeeze in two bedtime stories after you have both showered and brushed your teeth." Off they went to do their chores, hit the shower, and brush their teeth.

I trudged up the stairs and passed Judy coming down. She had inspected the shower results and listened to their prayers. I found two clean boys in their beds awaiting the stories. This was by far my favorite time of the day.

I asked the boys what book they wanted me to read but both boys shook their heads no. They said that from now on they wanted either a navy yarn, (sea story), or something from my childhood that I got in trouble for. I am not sure how they figured I got in so much trouble growing up.

I decided to tell them stories about teeth. Both boys had questioning looks on their faces. I told them how when I was a boy growing up, we lived with my grandparents' full time.

When my grandparents were growing up there wasn't much known about dentistry and so their teeth got a bunch of cavities and eventually all had to be removed. Both my grandparents had false teeth. These teeth they removed every night and put them in two coffee cups in the cupboard soaking in water. I was always an early riser and was often the first one up. My imaginary friend Joey and I were ALWAYS looking for a new adventure, I had discovered their teeth in the cupboard and decided to do an experiment, just like a scientist. First, I added salt to the water their teeth were sitting in. That morning at the breakfast table I watched them put their teeth in. They got this wild look in their eyes. They both reached for their orange juice and chugged it down. That was funny.

A few mornings later it was time for another experiment, so I added a little dishwashing soap to the water their teeth were sitting in. At the breakfast table they both began to spit. Grandpa even blew a bubble at the breakfast table. Mom says you aren't supposed to spit and NEVER at the table. Grandpa even blew a big bubble. All eyes focused on me as if I was the one that spit.

By now both my grandsons were laughing so loud I thought the neighbors would hear us. There was one more incident with the teeth and it happened one Saturday morning about a month later. Someone switched the teeth in the two cups. At the breakfast table that morning Grandpa ended up with Grandma's teeth and Grandma ended up with Grandpa's teeth. They plopped what they thought was their own teeth in their mouth, but they were NOT a match. Who knew?

As I headed down the stairs, I could still hear those boys laughing all the way down to the living room.

Grandma said, "Don't be filling those boys' impressionable minds with those kinds of stories."

CHAPTER 24

I looked in the paper and saw that the Montgomery baseball team, "The Biscuits," had a homestretch coming up. I called my friend who helped promote the team and made plans to take the boys to the ballpark that next afternoon. The team had a double header to play that day to make up for a game that had gotten rained out earlier that month.

At breakfast I told them our home team the Biscuits would be playing the Pensacola Blue Wahoo's. The boys laughed at the funny names. They wanted to know why they had never heard these teams before coming to Montgomery.

Once you graduate from college and if you are good enough you can get picked by one of the major league teams. Teams like the Yankees, and the Chicago Cubs. Playing professional baseball takes an awful lot of practice. Each of the professional teams sponsor what is called the farm club. There are three tiers in the farm club organization Single A, Double A, and Triple A, all called the minor leagues. Most players will spend some considerable time in the minor leagues honing their skills in the farm teams. They just weren't good enough to work their way up to the majors. Each major league team can only have 26 players on the team and as many as 40 on contract. Should a player get injured, and his recovery will be more than a couple of days, they move him down to the farm club until his injury heals and to sharpen his skills before heading back to the majors. The farm team acts as a source for reserve players. Some players never make it out of the farm teams and into the major league.

Our Biscuits are a double A ball club for the Tampa Bay Devil Rays.

"We need to leave early so we will arrive at the ballpark as the players are getting dressed and ready for the game. Here are a couple of baseballs each and a sharpie pen. If you are respectful and ask nicely you might get one of them to autograph a ball for you. Who knows if that player ends up famous you might have quite a valuable keepsake."

"One more thing we have to carry in with us," I said.

I grabbed a large paper bag from the kitchen counter as we walked to the truck and then drove to the stadium. We stopped at the security gate and gave our name to the guard. He sent us to the guard house and a lady gave us badges to wear.

The badges had big red letters that said VIP. The boys started laughing calling themselves the boys from VIP. Soon Pat Owens came down to meet us and we started our tour. The boys took turns using my cell phone to get pictures of themselves in the dug outs, the on-deck circle, and even taking some practice swings at home plate.

Harry said, "I can't wait to send these pictures to my team back in Illinois."

Mr. Owens said that the boys could run the bases if they wanted to. Of course, the boys took off like a pair of rockets. After they had rounded the bases three times, Pat led us to the locker rooms. Some of the players were already there. Each locker had a player's name and his uniform hung in his locker. Some lockers had pictures of their families and from some special fans.

I opened the paper sack Judy had prepared for our Biscuit players. I looked inside and there were her famous Apple Delight ice box cookies. I laid them out on the center table and suddenly there was a swarm of Biscuit players hovering to get their own piece of Apple Delight cookies. That this was not the first time these players had enjoyed Grandma's world-famous Apple Delight cookies was obvious.

There were a couple new additions to the team that hadn't been here the last time Grandma had baked cookies for the team. That was quickly remedied. Grandma's cookies were her idea of an ice breaker. We were instantly looked at as almost part of the team. In just a few minutes every one of those cookies were gone.

I said, "Looks like the cookies were a huge hit."

Harry chimed in with, "Grandma had really hit it out of the park with those cookies."

Everyone laughed.

Mr. Owens said that we needed to let the team get finished getting dressed so they can play ball. Our players had two games to win today.

CHAPTER 25

Mr. Owens took us into the owner's box, a room that had an unobstructed view of the field. It had several league trophies the team had won in a big display case. The windows overlooking the field were so clean that if it hadn't been for some biscuit stickers it would look like nothing was there. The box was centered directly behind home plate. If you were an owner, you had the best seats in the house.

On one wall of the room there was a big screen television and Mr. Owens showed us a digital slide presentation of the construction of the baseball field. It had started out as a train station then they added a matching wing at a right angle. The outside of the new wing matched the old wing of the train station so well that you couldn't tell where the old one left off and the new one began.

Mr. Owens said that the trains no longer stopped here and that the train station had been abandoned long ago. Fortunately, it hadn't been torn down. He pointed out that there were still train tracks that ran just past the home-run fence but along the Alabama river. If a train happened to be passing during game time the engineer, would give the trains loud horn a couple of blasts. Those blasts were so loud they could easily be heard throughout the entire stadium.

He went on to say that here at Biscuit stadium there was something VERY special about that train. If during a game a Biscuit player hit a home-run and that ball hit the train, one lucky fan would win a new car.

"Wow," the boys said at the same time.

Has it ever happened? They wanted to know.

Mr. Owens said, "So far they had given away four brand new automobiles."

Pat looked at his watch and said, "Well boys, time for you to get dressed. Harry looked at Shane, and Shane looked at Harry they both were dressed. "Oh, no," Pat said, you can't go out on the field during a game if you don't have on a Biscuit uniform. The boys looked shocked. They were led to a small dressing room and when they next reappeared, they were "Montgomery Biscuits" from the top of their head to the tip of their toes. They were then led down to field level and into the players dugout where they were soon joined by the rest of the Biscuit players.

Harry was the first to realize they were going to be "Bat Boy's" for the Biscuits. One of the base coaches took the boys aside and told them they were to key on him and only leave the safety of the dugout when he gave the signal. Their job was going to be collecting bats, shin guards, and gloves that players dropped during the game. They would take turns retrieving the bats and putting them in the proper slot that had the players number on it.

The boys did a super job being the Biscuit bat boys for the first game of the double header. The Biscuits pulled out a 3-2 win in the bottom of the 10th inning when a player stole home during a wild pitch. The boys were right there where all the action was.

After the game they were shown to a small locker room and told to wash their hands and faces and were then delivered to their grandfather, who had remained in the owner's box during the first game of the double header.

Mr. Owens was with him and said, "I bet you boys worked up quite an appetite out there on the field today."

We sure did they replied as one. Mr. Owens made a call and a waitress brought in two plates with footlong hotdogs and curly

French fries. One hot dog with ketchup and the other one with mustard. She also had two cokes for the boys.

I offered to pay for the food, but Pat would have no part of it. "I am just paying you and Judy back for last year," he said.

The boys' faces had that deer in the headlights look.

CHAPTER 26

Pat told the boys what had happened last year. During a powerful storm the wind had toppled a tree onto their house. He and his wife Lorraine had been pinned down by the tree. They couldn't get to a phone and Lorraine was seriously hurt. One of the sharp branches from the pine tree had gone through her upper leg.

Your grandfather was driving through the neighborhood looking for damage when he saw our house with a portion of the roof caved in and the top of a big pine tree going through it. He investigated and found me. Using a bow saw he kept in his truck soon had me cut out and back to the truck. From the odd shape of my arm, it was evident it was broken. He handed me his phone and had me call 911 and tell them we had an injured trapped woman and we needed help right away. The 911 operator said they would add our name to the list but that it would be a while. Your Grandfather went to the back of his truck, pulled out his first aid kit and went back in the house. He got down on his stomach crawled on the floor cutting branches along the way until he got to my wife. He put emergency bandages around her leg and the branch that had pierced her leg. Better to have the Dr's at the hospital remove that branch. He then cut the branch that had pierced her leg from the rest of the tree. Next he pulled her out by himself. Eased her out through the tunnel he had made going in. Once clear of the house he managed to get her over his shoulder and out to his truck. He carefully laid her down on the back seat and then raced us to the emergency room at the hospital.

The emergency room was packed but they had called in every one of the staff and soon were treating those injured by the storm. Due to my wife's injuries, they took her straight to the operating room where they removed the broken limb, cleaned her wound and set her broken leg in a cast. An hour later I joined her in her hospital room with my right arm in a cast and in a sling. What a pair we were. The doctor came in and informed us that we would both make a full recovery, but we were going to be sore for quite a spell and needed to spend a few days in the hospital.

That's when your grandfather stepped up to the plate once again, this time offering to help with the restoration and cleanup of our house. I thought why not? I didn't know this guy from Adam, but he had singlehandedly rescued my wife and me. We had already put our lives in his obviously capable hands. He went right to work, first contacting my insurance agent, then a guy he knew from his church who was in the tree removal business. He brought him by the hospital so I could meet him. A nice guy, his name was William Smith. He explained what he was going to do to remove the fallen tree from our house and that his crew would clean up the debris from the storm.

Your grandfather took a bunch of digital pictures which he forwarded to the insurance company. He even sent me a daily report so I could track the progress. Next thing I knew there was a fire truck showing up in some of the pictures. I called your grandfather to ask him why the firetruck and he informed me that he had convinced the local volunteer fire department they could use our damaged home as a training exercise. They spread a big tarp over the gaping hole in our roof to keep any rain out and causing more damage. He contacted a friend of his from the American Legion in town who happened to be a structural engineer. He had him look at the damage to the house and make repair recommendations.

He contacted a general contractor he knew, a man by the name of Jeremiah La Belle, brought him in and introduced us. He discussed the plan of action and said his crew would start on the repairs the very next week.

The hospital released me and planned on releasing my wife at the end of the week. Before I could contact the Glen Ridge Motel for a room, your grandfather insisted that I have dinner at his home. Your grandfather is a very persuasive man and he only had to mention your grandmother's Dutch apple pie and homemade vanilla ice cream and I was hooked for dinner.

I arrived for dinner and your grandmother insisted on showing me their beautiful home. She emphasized all the room they had and how there was a spare bedroom and bathroom on the ground floor with a separate entrance. "Why don't Marge and you stay here when she is released from the hospital. Stay there at least until she is out of the wheelchair and can navigate on crutches."

"If I thought your grandfather was persuasive, he couldn't hold a candle to your grandmother. Of course, that Dutch apple pie of hers really sealed the deal. To make a long story short we stayed with them for three weeks. Here we were complete strangers, and they just took us in like we were family. When Marge could navigate the crutches, we were able go back home. All the repairs were complete. Everything was done except for some outdoor painting and that was scheduled for the very next week."

"Things are always crazy during that time of the year, we are bringing in new ball players to replace those that have moved up to triple A baseball. Preseason ticket sales needed to start, and I really needed to be at work. I also needed to be home to take care of my wife. She was not a big fan of the crutches, and I was afraid she would fall. Your grandmother came over every morning just before I left for work and stayed with her.

"I was able to go back to work because your grandmother came over every day to spend it with her."

The boys and I watched the second game of the double header and Pat had his vendors deliver a piping hot pepperoni pizza for dinner.

I called Judy and told her not to hold supper for us. The boys held out until the seventh inning stretch and I could see the boy's eyes getting heavier and heavier. I told Pat I needed to get the boys home before they fell asleep at the ballpark. I thanked him for the awesome day he gave my grandsons.

He handed me two large envelopes and said wait until you are home to open them. He said the biscuit bat boy uniforms with their names on them were theirs to keep.

As we exited the stadium there was a golf-cart and driver who took us to the parking lot where my truck was parked.

I hadn't driven a mile until the boys were sound asleep in the back seat.

CHAPTER 27

The next morning at the breakfast table I let the boys open the envelopes Pat had given us. Each held six 8x10" photographs of them as bat boys the previous day.

The next few days the boys worked hard. They picked vegetables and berries in the mornings and sold them at their vegetable stand in the afternoon. Their grandmother would give them her order for what she would need from the garden for supper that evening, and they filled it first. They had a preview of what we were having for supper based on fulfilling their grandmother's request.

The next week the sweet corn was ready to pick. I rousted the boys up two hours earlier than usual so they could get the corn picked before it got too hot. If they thought their fruit and vegetable stand was busy before, it was nothing compared to when I added the fresh picked sweet corn to the sign. By three o'clock most of the fruits, vegetables, and all the sweet corn picked that morning were gone. Time to go swimming.

Their bank accounts continued to grow and each one had surpassed $500.00.

A routine began, pick the garden first thing in the morning, work the fruit stand until about 3, swim until supper time, listen to my navy yarns followed by dreams filled with adventures.

A couple more weeks until the county fair will be here. The county fair would start on Thursday and run until Sunday before they packed up and went to the next town. The boys could hardly wait. They told their grandmother that with the money they had saved they thought they could probably buy a snow cone trailer.

Advertisements for the fair were everywhere. I asked the boys if they would like to enter some of the contests for vegetables and berries. You would have thought I had offered them two tickets to the moon. The next morning, I joined them in the garden, and we decided which of the vegetables we would enter. I showed them what the judges would be looking for on each vegetable that was entered and then I let them choose which ones they wanted to enter. They finally understood it wasn't always the biggest vegetable that won the blue ribbons. An example, in the tomato category a smaller riper tomato would beat out a 1 lb. monster every time.

The boys learned things about vegetables that they never knew existed. Things like a bell pepper that has three lobes, or bumps on the bottom is a male, while a female bell pepper has four lobes on the bottom. A male bell pepper has fewer seeds and is less sweet than a female bell pepper. The female bell pepper is better to eat raw because of its sweeter flavor.

Finally, the day of the fair arrived, and the boys wanted to go to the bank and draw all their money out of their accounts. I was able to convince them that $50.00 was more than enough and that I would hold it until they saw something they really wanted to spend it on.

I explained to them that the county fair was really divided into four distinct areas. The exhibit area, the livestock area, the show area, and the midway. The midway had all the bright lights, fast moving rides, and games of chance that draw kids like flies to honey.

I explained to them we first had to drop our vegetables off to be judged. The judging would start at noon, we could come back at 4 and see how we did. Grandma had brought two pies to be judged and some of her strawberry jam.

I told the boys that after we dropped off the vegetables, we would head over to the livestock area and see all the animals up close. I explained that just like our vegetables were being judged so were the livestock. The livestock belonged to kids who were members of the 4 H club.

I could see that neither of the boys were familiar with the 4H club.

I told them that 4-H is a youth program where adult volunteers provide, hands-on, fun, and educational opportunities with youth ages 5 to 19. This can take place in many different settings such as project clubs, community clubs, after school programs, camps, workshop, or events. 4-H provides youth the opportunities to succeed and learn new experiences to help them become productive, successful adults.

Several 4-H kids were grooming their animals before going in front of the judges. I forgot what 4-H stands for, and suggested asking that girl that is brushing her calf's hide to a glossy shine.

Harry introduced himself, and the girl said her name was Sally. He said he wasn't from here and could she tell him what the 4-H means.

She put down her brush and said, "Sure. The first "H" in 4-H stands for Head; Head to clearer thinking.

"The second "H" in 4-H stands for Heart; Heart to greater loyalty.

"The next "H" in 4-H stands for Hands; Hands for larger service.

"4-H'ers are busy with their hands all year long learning new things and caring for their projects with hands-on experiences.

"The last "H" in 4-H stands for Health; "Health to better living. Knowing how to cook and grow food, and appreciating art allows 4-H'ers to gain an understanding of how the world works and how to live healthy."

"Wow," Shane said, "that sounds an awful lot like scouting."

"In some ways it is," Sally said, "but it is a lot more hands on. For example, I was there when my calf Buttercup was born, I got to help the veterinarian clean her after she was born. With help from my dad, we got her to nurse from her mom the first time. Every day after school it was my job to look after Buttercup and for the first 3 months while Buttercup was nursing, her mom too. I had to clean out the stall, put fresh straw for them to lie on, supply fresh water to drink and fresh hay to eat."

"I thought taking care of a dog took a lot of time," Shane chimed in.

"When spring came, I gathered big bundles of clover and fed them to Buttercup. They were her favorites. Well, they were her favorites until the day I forgot to latch the gate properly and ran to catch the school bus."

"What happened?" Shane asked.

"Buttercup decided she would investigate our vegetable garden. Turns out she liked our vegetables even more than she liked clover. What she was most fond of was my dad's prize pumpkin. He was going to enter it in the fair this year. He was kind of mad until mom reminded him, he had never won the giant pumpkin contest before, and was more than likely not going to win it this year either."

CHAPTER 28

Next, I took the boys to the midway, I could see they could hardly wait to spend their money on the games of chance. Before I gave them a single dollar to spend, I suggested we first walk around to find which games they wanted to play and to see if they could identify how the games could be rigged.

There was the basketball hoop game where you had five tries to make three baskets to win a prize. If you got four baskets, you won a giant prize and if you made all five you got the grand prize. Both boys told me they were pretty good at making foul shots at school and they thought they could get three out of five to win a prize. I asked them if they wanted to cheat people what could they do to make the game even harder?

Shane said, "You could make the hoop smaller."

Harry said, "or the basketball bigger."

Or they could know that the standard basketball hoop is 10 feet high. If people practiced at home and got good at making basketball free throws if they changed the height of the rim either up or down that would throw someone's aim way off.

We watched the next 10 customers. Only one guy won a general prize with three baskets. It took him three turns to win that. I then asked the boys how much they thought the general prize was worth and they agreed on $2.00. He had spent $9.00 to win a $2.00 toy. He probably wouldn't have spent more than the first $2.00 if he hadn't been egged on by the man who ran the game. He kept taunting the high school kid who wanted to show off to his girlfriend. Both boys noticed that the guy who ran this game had a big snake tattoo running up his arm and coming out by his neck. It made him look evil.

The rest of the 10 customers had won nothing from the snake man and he had collected $36.00 giving away only $2.00 in merchandise. That is a very healthy profit.

The next game we looked at was to toss a softball into a milk jug. The milk jug was close, you could hardly miss. Again, we watched some people play. It looked easy, but no one was winning. I asked the boys, "if you wanted to cheat people on the game what could you do?"

Both boys agreed, "make the hole in the top of the milk can smaller than it appears." Sure, enough several people had tossed what looked like perfect tosses only to watch their softball bounce out at the last minute.

One by one we went up one side and down the other side looking at the games of chance. Soon the boys became experts at finding the tricks behind the games which cheated people.

Behind the rows of the carnival games, we saw trailers where the people lived while the fair was in town. Just as we turned the corner, I saw two teenagers exit a trailer and pick up two giant grand prizes. I told the boys we would follow those teenagers for a little bit and to see where they were going and what they were up to. The two teens started wandering the midway telling all the people where they had won those giant grand prizes and how easy it was. Several people were sent in the direction of the recommended carnival game, only to lose their money as well. I explained to the boys that what those teenagers were is what is known as a Shill. A Shill is an accomplice of a hawker, gambler, or swindler who acts as an enthusiastic customer to entice or encourage others.

I then asked the boys what games they wanted to play and give their hard-earned money. The boys looked dejected and admitted they didn't want to give their money to any of them.

Lesson learned, I smiled to myself.

"Grandpa, how do you know so much about the games at the fair?" Shane asked.

"I too was once taken by the people who work the carnival games, and they took my hard-earned money. I brought $5.00 of my worm selling money to the carnival on a Friday night. The game I fancied was shooting targets with corks from a cork gun. The prize I had my eye on was a shiny new fishing knife in a sheath."

"I spent my entire $5.00 and didn't win a thing. My Grandpa had let me shoot his bb gun and he said I was a pretty good shot. When I complained to him, he told me that all the games at carnivals and fairs were good for one thing and one thing only, separating hard working people from their hard-earned money."

"I didn't want to believe my grandfather that there were people out there who wanted to cheat others on purpose. So, I went back the next day with another $5.00 of my worm selling business savings. This time I stood back and just watched for a while."

"There was a long line, and I was watching the shooters that were ahead of me. Some shooters, their shots went wide left, and some went wide right. It happened despite the shooters claiming they had sighted it in perfectly. When I had worked my way up to the front of the line, I got the gun that was shooting too far to the left. I purposely aimed to the right of my intended target and sure enough the cork flew true and took down target number one. Four more shots and I had five targets down. I could choose any prize I wanted. I chose the knife. The man working the game refused to let me try again, handed me my knife, and sent me on my way. The knife turned out to be junk. It broke a few days later."

CHAPTER 29

"Let's go get an ice cream cone," I said.

Both boy's eyes lit up like Christmas trees. Then they asked if they could have a corn dog too. Of course, I said yes. Besides, their grandmother wasn't here to override me. She hated all carnival food. I told the boys that this carney food was between us men.

They nodded their heads and Shane said, "Don't worry grandpa, we have your back."

While we were eating the ice cream cones, I told the boys that when the fair comes to town the crime in the area goes way up. I spoke to our Sheriff Burt Kaper, and he has put his officers on overtime to try and keep the robberies in the area down while the carnival is in town. The carnival is a perfect place for thieves to hideout pretending to be fair workers during the hours the fair is open and then sneaking into town and stealing whatever isn't nailed down. He gets a list of who is traveling with the fair and he says almost every worker has a criminal record and been arrested for one thing or another. They are in an area for such a short period of time then they are gone to the next town or maybe the next state by the time the local people find out they have been robbed.

We met grandma back at the exhibit area. Most of the entries had been judged and the boys could collect several blue and red ribbons for their entries. Grandma got a blue ribbon for her apple pie and her strawberry jam. When I asked her what about the berry pie she laughed, that wasn't for judging that was for eating, sort of, she laughed.

Just then the announcer called everyone's attention to the two tables at the back of the exhibit hall. Sitting down at the table were the Mayor, the High School Principal, and the head of the hospital. Sitting in front of each one of them was a pie. They were going to have a pie eating contest to raise money for a new x-ray machine at the hospital. They had a big fishbowl up front, and people were asked to make donations. I reached for my wallet and put twenty dollars in. I saw both boys whispering to one another, coming to agreement and then telling me they wanted to contribute their $50.00 to this good cause. That gesture brought tears to this grandfather's eyes. When it looked like all the money had been donated that was going to be donated, the head of the hospital thanked everyone and introduced the three "pie eaters".

He then thanked the women by name who donated the pies. My wife beamed when they called out her name. The contestants were all dressed in a white T-shirt. He then said that each man's wife was standing behind her man to give him words of encouragement. Their grandmother whispered to the boys that she had spoken to all the ladies who had baked the pies and they were all berry pies and would look great spread all over those white t-shirts. He said when the air horn sounded each contestant would start eating his pie without using their hands. The contest would be over when the air horn sounded a second time.

The air horn went off and all three men dove into their pies. Grandma was laughing her head off and was rooting for the mayor because he had gotten her pie. What a mess those three people were. From my own experience they might just as well toss those T shirts in the trash because those berry stains would never come out no matter how many times you washed them. A few minutes later the air horn sounded and the men stopped eating their pies. The judge then asked the contestants wives to hold the pies up so the crowd could see which one had eaten the most and as soon as they lifted them they pushed the pies in their husbands faces. Everyone broke out in laughter, well everyone except the mayor, the principal, and the hospital president. The announcer said, looks like we have a 3-way tie.

Just then the local newspaper photographer snapped their pictures for the next edition of "The Evening Telegram".

We headed home, the boys took a quick shower while grandma made them a toasted cheese sandwich. The boys had had another full day.

CHAPTER 30

The next morning the boys called their parents and told of all their adventures so far. Their moms both asked them if they were having a good time and Harry said, "No, we are having a GREAT time."

Both boys shared with their parents about their trip to the Biscuits field, their time they spent being bat boys, their fishing trip, last night at the fair, how great a cook their grandmother was, their fruit and vegetable stand, and the savings accounts they had opened up. Harry's dad asked if they had any time to sleep. After the phone call I broke the news to the boys it was vegetable picking time and time to open their vegetable stand. We were going to shut it down around noon because I had a special adventure for them. Both boys ran out of the back door like their coat tails were on fire. They grabbed their berry baskets and a wheelbarrow and to the garden they went.

After a lunch of cucumber sandwiches, I told them to put on their dirtiest and oldest clothes. They looked at me as if I had fallen off the turnip truck. When the boys got to the truck, they expected their grandmother was going to send them both back in the house to change clothes. Instead, she looked them up and down, and nodded her head in approval. The boys hopped in the truck, and we headed back to the fair. The boys commented that it looked much different in the light of day.

We went to the livestock barn, where they had one section walled off with bales of hay. All laid out was a racecourse and today the racers were young piglets. Each one had a number and his or her own rooting section. We were sitting in the green section. All at once the barrier was dropped and the piglets ran along the course trying to reach the prize at the end, a big feed trough of shelled corn. Somehow the piglets must have known ahead of time what the reward was because the race was over in just a couple of seconds. There were six races to determine which pigs would be entered in the final race. The 4-H kids who owned the pigs that finished in the first three places got trophies as well as ribbons and their pictures taken for the paper.

The next thing I wanted the boys to witness was the greased pole contest. The announcer informed the spectators that he had personally tacked a new $100.00 bill to the top of that pole. The pole had been stripped of all the bark, one end was buried deep in a hole, and then coated with about ten pounds of grease. He then opened to all challengers the opportunity to climb up the pole and grab that $100.00 bill and take it home.

Both my grandsons stood up thinking this was why I wanted them in old clothes. I shook my head no and told them to sit back down. They watched as some high school aged kids gave it a try only to slide back down the pole. The crowd booed and cheered them on at the same time. Next some older men gave it a try and the same thing happened. The high school kids gave it another try but had the same results. Then a man who must have been the same age as I am huddled the boys and young men together and whispered a plan. Together the men and the high school boys worked together and made a pyramid with the bigger people on the bottom and the lighter ones on top. In that way they were able to retrieve the prize at the top of the pole.

The boy's Grandmother said, "Those fools, by the time they divide up the winnings there won't be enough to replace the clothes they ruined, mercy me."

While we had been watching the greased pole contest, they had rearranged the bales of straw so there was a large open area. I took the boys over to the starting area where they were joined by twelve other kids ages 10-12.

Their Grandmother called the boys over and whispered something in their ears, they looked down at the ground but nodded respectfully.

The next thing you heard was the squealing of a pig. Before releasing the pig, a large amount of grease was applied to the entire pig. Then the kids were released, and every kid tried to catch that pig. The problem was, that pig didn't want to be caught.

Sometimes the squeals of the pig drowned out the squeals of the kids and sometimes the squeals of the kids was louder than the pigs. Just when a couple of kids would think they had the pig cornered it would dash between one of their legs and take off. A couple times I thought Harry had a good hold on one of the legs when it slipped his grip, and another time Shane tackled the pig only to be drug across the ground for ten feet before the pig slipped his grip. After about twenty minutes the pig ran out of steam and two of the other boys worked together and captured the pig.

Everyone was still laughing 15 minutes later. My side hurt so much from laughing at my grandsons I thought I was going to have to call an ambulance and have them take me to the hospital. When I had the boys alone, "I asked them what their grandmother had whispered to them just before the greased pig contest."

The boys looked at each other, shrugged their shoulders and in unison they said, "Don't you catch that pig. If you catch that pig, there will be no more desserts the rest of your stay."

That kind of attitude cost me some good bacon and sausage, but it did confirm we would have plenty of Grandma's desserts while the boys were here.

CHAPTER 31

We headed back to the truck, and I spread out a big blue plastic tarp and had the boys ride back there for the short ride home. Judy went to the kitchen and grabbed a big bottle of dishwashing soap, and I led the boys out to the shed where clean clothes and new sneakers awaited their degreasing.

I told the boys, "Dishwashing liquid was the best thing to use to get the grease off your body because it was gentle on your skin and designed to remove grease."

The fair would be leaving town on Sunday headed somewhere closer to Atlanta. It was fine with me; the boys had learned quite a bit about what goes on behind the flashing lights and fast talk of the carneys. Hopefully they would never get suckered in by people like that. Once the carnival left town and things got back to normal, I was planning on taking the boys fishing a couple more times, take in another Biscuits baseball game or two, and maybe teach them the role Alabama played in the civil war. I might take them on a tour of the first White House of the Confederacy in Montgomery. I still wanted them to learn more about the underground railroad and Daniel Pratt, Prattville's founder.

After the boys were degreased and in clean clothes, I took them downtown and showed them the big brick factory. I explained that Daniel Pratt had built it along the Autauga creek, to manufacture cotton gins.

I explained to the boys that when they look at cotton growing in the field each one of those white puffs of cotton has seeds which are difficult and labor intensive to remove. The cotton gin removed the seeds mechanically and quickly.

This cotton gin led to an increase in the production of cotton. The landowners grew wealthier than ever before.

PART II

CHAPTER 32

Kathy Sweet is a 10-year-old girl moving from a big city in Arizona to a small city in Alabama. Her family is moving because of her dad's new job. She's a bit of a tom boy because of her two older brothers. Her brothers were lucky enough to stay behind during this house hunting trip, staying with her dad's parents so they can go to football camp. When football camp is over, and her parents had found a new place to live, they would be joining the rest of the family in Alabama. The boys had only one request for the new house, they wanted one with a swimming pool in the backyard.

Kathy is the youngest of her family. She is NOT happy about going to a new school and leaving all her friends behind. She does not want to be the new kid in school and have everybody make fun of her because she doesn't talk like them, or eat the same kind of food, or wear the latest clothes. The only concession her parents made to ease the transition for their daughter was they had gotten her an Apple iPhone.

Kathy and her parents have a month to find a place to live in Alabama, and Her dad has two months before his new job at GE starts. The plant he would be working at was a big GE Plastics Plant located just outside of Montgomery, Alabama.

Her dad had been in contact with the HR department at his new job location and they had recommended a town called Prattville because it has a better school system.

Her mom was trying to paint a pretty picture of how exciting a new place would be, but Kathy had her doubts. She had searched the internet about Montgomery, and it seemed like every restaurant had barbecue somewhere in its name. She knew that when she visited her grandparents in Texas they claimed the best barbecue in the whole world. Kathy liked barbecue but didn't want it morning, noon, and night.

For some reason ever since they crossed the border into Texas, Kathy's mom and dad thought they were country western singers. Her dad always said he liked both kinds of music, country and western.

They had the radio station tuned to every country station they could find. Thank God, she had her new iPhone and ear buds.

One of the searches she did on the internet about things to do near Prattville was to go fishing. She loved going fishing with her dad. Her dad realized that he wasn't spending enough time with her. To fix that he gave her his undivided attention for one Saturday a month. Just the two of them 7 AM to 7 PM to do whatever fun things she wanted to do. It started with breakfast out and from there, maybe to the mall, to go see a movie double feature, and sometimes going fishing. The article she read said they had catfish farms open to the public. She couldn't wait to go fishing with her dad. She wasn't too sure how you farmed catfish, but she was looking forward to it. She planned on trying that out just as soon as they could get their stuff unpacked and she could get her dad away from work.

Kathy had decided that she would journal her trip. When she got settled, she would do her own blog about their trip. She had decided she was not going to let them off the hook for moving just because they had gotten her this cool, iPhone and ear buds. She decided she would play this for all it was worth.

Her parents soon realized there was an added benefit to her having her own iPhone and ear buds. It made traveling 1700 miles from Phoenix, Az to Prattville, Al a whole lot more peaceful since the iPhone kept her entertained most of the drive.

Her dad was always trying to make family car trips entertaining as well as educational. He had the whole trip planned. Our first stop was my mom's parents' house in Texas. We spent two days with grandparents and then it was off on her dad's GREAT ADVENTURE plan. He promised the plan would be fun, but the jury is still out.

First stop the Alamo.

CHAPTER 33

They stopped at the Alamo in San Antonio, Texas. If her dad hadn't explained to her all about the Alamo, she would have just thought it was an old run-down building. He explained that it was originally a Spanish mission built to teach the local American Indians.

She had looked up the Alamo on the internet and thought it was a rental car company. She told that to her dad and he and mom both laughed. She then looked it up on her new iPhone and found out that the Alamo they were going to visit was the remains of an old mission that played a vital role during Texas' war for independence from Mexico. She never realized that Texas used to be part of Mexico.

Her dad said, "Alamo's 200 defenders–commanded by James Bowie and William Travis and including the famed frontiersman Davy Crockett—held out for 13 days before the Mexican forces numbering in the thousands finally overpowered them.

"It was a delaying action which allowed Sam Houston the time to raise a proper army to face Santa Anna. The Battle of the Alamo became a lasting symbol of their resistance to Mexican rule and their struggle for Texas independence. The battle cry of "remember the

Alamo" is a rallying cry that is today uttered by men going into battle."

She wondered why her history teachers can't teach history like her dad. He makes it so interesting and easy to remember. She doesn't think she will ever forget the story of the Alamo.

CHAPTER 34

The next stop on their journey was in Waco Texas. They planned on spending a few days there. Her mom was so excited because her dad had reserved a two-night stay at the Magnolia House. Whatever that was.

Mom said someone named Chip and Joanna Gaines had been stars on a television show called "Fixer Upper". They had introduced Magnolia House on their Christmas show. They had taken an old rundown house and they transformed the historic home into a charming bed and breakfast vacation rental. Her mom said she had watched every show during the transformation. All mom did was "ooh" and "ahh" about all the furnishings in the bed and breakfast. I think if Chip and or Joanna had shown up, she would have asked them for their autograph. That would have been so embarrassing. It really wasn't my thing it was just stuff, but Mom sure liked it.

The second night in Waco, Dad took us on a spooky tour of Waco. Dad had signed us up with a tour group. They drove us to see the city's famous haunts and hear the legends behind them. Our guide told us some of the history about Waco and how a tornado paid a visit in the 1950s and wiped out most of the town.

The guide told us all about the haunted houses, and just as we were passing an old cemetery, He told us about a gunfight which took place just on the other side of the high stone fence surrounding the cemetery. The gun fight was over a woman. Both men were killed. Even today some evenings, people claim, pistol shots can be heard as each ghost tries to win the gunfight and come back to the living.

Just then behind the cemetery fence we could see two figures facing each other. Next, we heard two gunshots and both men fell to the ground. I jumped into my dad's lap, only to find my mother had gotten there first. My heart was beating a mile a minute. Several people on the tour let out a scream, I think I was one of them.

After a moment the tour guide laughed and said, "Don't worry. They were not gun shots just some firecrackers to bring some realism into the tour."

As far as my mom and I were concerned they can keep the realism, they scared us half to death.

We got back to Magnolia house and dad said," Tomorrow we will be going to the museum of the Texas Rangers." I went to sleep thinking about the Texas Rangers. My iPhone said it was a baseball team. Who wants to go visit a baseball team?

CHAPTER 35

The next day I learned a valuable lesson when looking things up on my iPhone. The first thing that shows up when doing a search may not be what you are really looking for. Come to find out, the Texas Ranger museum we were going to visit had nothing to do with the Texas Ranger baseball team. Our tour guide met us at the entrance of the Texas Ranger Museum and explained that when settlers from the early United States first came to Texas there was no regular army or even police force to protect them. They called the citizens together and organized a group to provide the needed protection. They first referred to this group as the Rangers. The name seemed very fitting, for their duties required them to range over the entire state of Texas. The name the Texas Rangers stuck.

Her dad read from the travel guide that Texas is a big state and initially it was patrolled by only 25 men entirely on horseback. On November 24, 1835, they passed an ordinance providing for three companies of Rangers, 56 men to the company, each commanded by a captain, first and second lieutenants, with a major in command. The privates received $1.25 per day for "pay, rations, clothing, and horse service," and the enlistment was for one year. The Rangers acted to protect the settlements against raiding Indians while Sam

Houston and his army defeated the troops of Santa Anna in the Battle of San Jacinto on April 21, 1836.

After the Texas Revolution, and up to 1840, the Texas

Rangers were used principally for protection against the Indians.

Over the years the Texas Rangers transformed themselves into a state police force.

When a Ranger was going to meet an outside enemy, for example, the Indians or the Mexicans. He was very close to being a soldier. However, when he had to chase down to the enemies within his own society - outlaws, train robbers, and highwaymen, he was a detective and police officer.

The Rangers' duties were not limited by city or county boundaries but included the whole state. Generally, the Ranger gets called in when a case is considered too great for a local agency.

The museum was filled with the actual weapons many of the Texas Rangers used every day. The many photographs, citations, and awards proved the Texas Rangers were a very tough group of men. Most lived on horseback and carried everything they owned tied to their saddle or in their saddle bags.

An old movie was about one special guy called the "Lone Ranger". Dad made a big deal out of it because he had watched the movie back when he was a boy.

He said our next stop was going to be in Louisiana and to prepare ourselves for a special treat.

CHAPTER 36

The next morning, we ate a big breakfast at the Magnolia house and prepared ourselves for the next part of our journey. Dad said it would be about a four-hour drive to our next adventure. I must have fallen asleep because when I awoke, we were pulling into "Ragin Cajun Bayou Tours."

Dad had arranged for us to go on one of those airboat rides through the swamps. He just HAD to see an Alligator up close and personal. He had watched way too many episodes of Swamp People.

I am sure mom had put her foot down or he would have us going on one of those Gator capture boats, yuck.

They had five boats, and they were all called "Ragin Cajun" and numbered 1-5. We had to read and sign a release form stating we understood that there were risks involved and should we be eaten by an alligator or drown because the boat sank, we couldn't hold them responsible. We were introduced to our Captain and tour guide for the day, he said his name was Captain Ron. He explained that we had originally been assigned to Ragin Cajun boat number 6 but that it hadn't come back from the last group of tourists it had taken out to the swamp.

My mom asked him when they were due back and Captain Ron said, "Last Tuesday."

My mom looked panicked when she said," last Tuesday was 3 days ago."

Captain Ron said, "Don't worry they would eventually turn up."

My mom asked my dad, "Are you sure about this Robert."

To which he replied, "Margret it will be a blast, You will love it. Trust me."

I must admit I wasn't too clear on what a swamp boat was, and our captain quickly corrected me and said it was properly called an air boat. If like me, you're wondering what, exactly, is an airboat?

Airboats were initially used as a means of navigating shallow waters, like those in these Louisiana swamps and the Florida Everglades, so that people could fish and hunt. Airboats are the best way to travel on water because the water is too shallow for a standard submerged propeller engine. Airboats are different in that they have a flat bottom and move with the help of a large, caged propeller on the back of the boat. Eventually airboats became a large part of the tourism business, especially here in the Louisiana bayou and the Florida Everglades.

Captain Ron said, "Riding an airboat is an exciting way for you and your family to see the wildlife that live in the swamps."

I must give my dad some credit, the airboat ride was a lot more fun than I could have ever dreamed of. We saw Alligators, egrets, turtles, eagles, and nutria. I didn't know what a nutria was, but Captain Ron explained it looked like a cross between a beaver and a big rat. Nutria was introduced into Washington for the fur-farming industry in the 1930s.

Captain Ron said, "A nutria will eat 25 percent of its body weight each day. Unfortunately, because it eats the roots and stems of plants, it destroys about ten times more plant matter than it eats. They turn shoreline areas into muddy bogs, destroying marshes that provide protection for flooding and habitat for other animals.

The captain was very entertaining and at one point he left the airboat and got down on his hands and knees and kissed an alligator. Mom said the alligator was probably fake or dead and then the alligator opened its mouth to get a treat that Captain Ron tossed into his open mouth. So much for it being fake or dead.

Dad asked Captain Ron if he could feed the alligator but before he could answer him Mom said, "I don't think so Robert."

I was glad I had taken Captain Ron's advice and put my hair in a ponytail and then into one of their $11.95 Ragin Cajun ball caps they had for sale. I sure didn't want my hair to get sucked into the big fan that pushed the boat through the swamp. Captain Ron promised me he would autograph the cap when we got back, free of charge.

The air boat ride was tons of fun. As promised Captain Ron signed my hat and I now have a souvenir I can show my brothers. Our journey east continued.

CHAPTER 37

Dad said, "Our next stop is Memphis, Tennessee. It is only slightly off our travel path, and it would be a shame to be this close to the birthplace of the Blues and not stop in. Of course, I didn't know a thing about "The Blues." I had heard of feeling blue as in sad, but music called "The Blues" was completely new to her.

Once again, my new iPhone came to the rescue. I looked up the blues and quickly learned that Blues music is characterized by sad melodies. The expression 'having the blues' means you are feeling gloomy. Early blues music was very slow and emotional, using simple harmonies with a vocalist accompanied by a guitar.

I wasn't sure that this was something I would like, but my dad had been right on target so far. I might just as well give it a try. At least it wasn't country or western.

My Dad said, "We will be getting up pretty early, having a big breakfast, and then spending the day on a tour bus. They will show us the sights and tell us all about the role Memphis played in the careers of famous musicians that changed music forever."

As promised her dad got them up early the next morning, so early the hotel didn't have breakfast ready yet.

He said, "Not to worry he hadn't planned on us eating breakfast there."

We left the hotel and halfway down the block there was a small restaurant called "Waffle House". Dad said you couldn't consider yourself a true southerner until you ate at this chain restaurant. He said the restaurant chain was everywhere in the south. He kidded us that there were no locks on the door because they never closed.

Even at 5AM there were quite a few people in the restaurant. My mom said they looked like a rough group, and perhaps we should find another restaurant. My dad said this was the only place open this time of the morning, and we wouldn't be here very long.

As we were walking to a table in back, one of the men sitting at the counter spun around on his stool and watched me the whole way. He had a giant snake tattooed on his arm that went in his shirt sleeve and shown its head and fangs on his neck. He didn't say anything and all he did was smile the whole time, but he scared me.

We took a seat and a waitress rushed over to our table to hand out menus, bring my parents a hot cup of coffee and a glass of orange juice for me. We decided to take her advice and started our morning with a special of the Waffle House, pecan waffles. They were excellent. The waitress that took the order spoke in some kind of code to the guy doing the cooking. Somehow, he knew what the code was. Within 15 minutes they had our order ready, and it was served steaming hot right off the griddle. We finished breakfast, went back to our hotel and packed, then got in the car and went to the parking lot for the bus tour.

CHAPTER 38

We met the tour guide and surrendered our tickets as we boarded the bus. This bus was a much nicer bus than school busses were. There were comfortable seats, and nobody was yelling, or pushing, or throwing things. The bus even had its own restroom in back, which I was sure I would NOT be using.

As soon as the final passengers had boarded the bus, the driver closed the door, and a young woman who had a microphone introduced herself as our tour guide. Next, she introduced our bus driver, she said, "His name was Ralph. It wasn't his real name but had been given him by many of the previous tour bus riders."

Just about everyone on the bus started laughing. I didn't get it. By the look on my face, my dad knew I didn't get it, so he leaned over and whispered in my ear that "Ralph" is another way of saying he made those people throw up.

"How gross," I replied.

The guide said her name was Mary Jane but if we forgot her name she would also answer to "Hey You," everybody laughed. While looking at a group of 10 gray haired men who must have all been at least in their 70's, she said, "if there were any cute single guys on board. I will be giving each one of them my contact information and a list of my favorite restaurants in the Memphis area."

Everyone laughed even more, especially the older guys who I later learned were from a Veterans of Foreign Wars, (VFW) post from Maryland. She started out by telling us the tour would last about 6 hours and would return right back here where our cars were parked.

Dad said, "I can tell it is going to be a good tour just based on the tour guide." He explained that her introduction and the way she kidded around with the older guys was called an ice breaker.

Mary Jane explained that we couldn't have chosen a better time to take this tour because 2022 marks the 45th anniversary of Elvis' passing. His legacy is just as diverse as it was relevant 45 years later. He has new fans experiencing his music for the first time that continue to add to his loyal following. A following that still echoes within the walls of Graceland. This year celebrates the man, the legend, the King of Rock 'n' Roll.

I had heard of Elvis before, but I had never taken the time to listen to his music. We pulled off the road and into a covered parking lot, the tour guide said they had one more passenger to pick up. The bus doors opened and a flashy guy wearing white bell bottom pants and a tight white shirt got on the bus. Then he started singing, "One for the money, two for the show, three to get ready and go cat go." He sang the song, "Don't step on my blue suede shoes and Love me Tender." He exited the bus as quickly as he had entered. The tour guide was laughing and told us we had just been visited by the "King of Rock n Roll," Elvis. I thought that maybe my iPhone and I would look up some of his music the next time my parents were singing another country western song. She asked her mom and dad if they were Elvis fans when they were growing up?

Her dad said, "It was before my time, you will have to ask your mother." Her mom playfully socked him in the arm. Her dad was constantly making fun of the fact that mom was 18 months older than he was.

Her Mom said, "Now Kathy, think for a minute, you now know

that Elvis has been dead for 45 years. Just how old do you think we are?"

Her dad jumped in quickly and said, "Kathy don't answer that." They all had a great laugh.

CHAPTER 39

Mary Jane told them the first stop we would be making was the birthplace of Elvis, it was in Tupelo, Mississippi. When we pulled up, everyone on the bus seemed to be amazed how small his house was. It looked like their shed out behind the house in Phoenix. Mary Jane told them it was a shotgun style house. She explained for those of you that aren't familiar with a shotgun style house it means it was a straight shot from the front door to the back door. A lot of chuckles could be heard on the bus, especially from the VFW guys. She also told them at the site they would find a museum, a chapel, and the Assembly of God Church building where the Presley family worshipped. The bus would remain there for 30 minutes for those that wanted to get out and stretch their legs or go into the Elvis house, the chapel, or the small museum, for a closer look.

As soon as everyone was back on the bus "Ralph" turned the bus around and we headed back towards Memphis. Mary Jane got back on the microphone and told us that as humble as his birthplace was, he didn't live there long. His parents were forced to move out of the shotgun house when Elvis was just a few years old because they couldn't pay the rent. His parents were very poor. They moved several times during the 13 years they lived in Mississippi.

Mary Jane said, "Time to stop thinking about Elvis and his 45-year-old legacy and talk about the Blues. They say the best journeys are the ones that take us home, and that couldn't be more fitting for the followers of the Mississippi Blues Trail. After all, most of today's popular music finds its roots in the blues, a type of music that was born right here in Mississippi.

This journey starts with our next stop, the city of Cleveland, Mississippi at Dockery Farms, which is widely believed to be the actual birthplace of the blues. When Charley Patton was playing tunes at all-night picnics and teaching guitar to musicians, they called him the "Howlin' Wolf". There are over 200 trail markers that point to other landmarks of the blue's movement around the state. Some of the most unique include the Clarksdale crossroads where Robert Johnson, supposedly sold his soul to the devil in exchange for guitar-playing wizardry. The birthplace of B.B. King is only a short jaunt from the late performer's award-winning museum in Indianola. For those of you that have worked up an appetite you will be happy to know we will be having lunch at the historic Blue Front Café in Bentonia."

CHAPTER 40

Cheers rang up from the passengers, but especially from the VFW guys.

As we pulled up to the café, I couldn't believe what I was seeing. It was a concrete block building and the front of it was painted blue. Both my Mom and I looked at one another and our minds were saying the same thing. "We aren't going to eat here."

Her dad spoke up and said, "It probably looks a lot better on the inside than it does on the outside"

Mom said, "It will have to."

Dad said, "I don't think the bus tour company would have this on our itinerary if it wasn't safe to eat here. I am going to follow Mary Jane's lead, if she thinks it is safe enough to eat here, I will eat here, besides I am starving."

Mom said, "How can you be starving with that breakfast you put away? When we get settled in our new home you are going on a diet."

This was NOT the first-time mom had put dad on a diet and more than likely it wouldn't be the last.

They walked in the Blue Front Café, and as if her dad had been here before, he was exactly right. It was completely different on the inside. There were all these shiny autographed guitars hanging on the walls and the place was clean. It looked like a museum. Some wonderful aromas were coming from the kitchen.

Mary Jane told us that the guitars hanging on the walls were autographed by their owners and considered priceless.

We sat down and looked at the menu. After about 5 minutes the waiter came to the table to take our order. Dad said he would have a cup of jambalaya soup, a barbecue sandwich, and some coleslaw.

I felt I had eaten enough barbecue to last me a lifetime, so I was happy when I saw cheeseburgers on the menu. I ordered a cheeseburger extra pickle, French fries, and a coke.

Mom got a salad and a cup of a soup called Jambalaya. She took a spoonful and said it was very spicy.

I was the first one done with my lunch and decided I wanted to get a picture of the guitars hanging on the wall. Using the camera on my iPhone I thought they would make a great addition for my blog. I then went outside to get a picture of the front of the famous Blue Front Café.

As I was heading out the door my dad said, "Don't wander off, the bus will be leaving soon, and we don't want to have to look for you."

I thought like, "Where am I going to go?"

I had just taken a picture of the Blue Front Café with the camera feature on my iPhone when a guy came up and asked me if I wanted him to take my picture standing in front of the café. I told him sure. I handed over my phone. He said it would be a better picture if I stood near the corner and that way, he could get me and the entire front of the Blue Front Café.

I got to the corner of the building and then somebody put a rough bag over my head. A hand closed over the bag and closed over my mouth so I couldn't yell. I started to kick and struggle to get free. I then felt a prick in my arm, the person behind me muffled my mouth with part of the bag. I heard the sliding door of a van door open; I seemed to be getting very tired; my legs didn't want to hold me up anymore.

Child Trafficking and the Underground Railroad

The last thing I heard before I was thrown in the van and everything went dark was someone say, "lose the phone, they can track those things."

CHAPTER 41

When I awoke, I was no longer in the bag they had put over my head, instead they had what looked like a whole roll of duct tape around my ankles and wrists and even a piece across my mouth. I wondered what was happening to me. Where were my mom and dad? Tears began to roll down my cheeks all by themselves. Where was she and who were these three men.

When one of them noticed I was awake he came and knelt over her. She noticed the big snake tattoo on his arm. She had seen that before. He was one of the men she had seen at the Waffle House where she and her parents had eaten breakfast.

He said, "Look kid, we can do this the hard way or the easy way. You need to face reality and understand that you belong to us. No amount of crying or yelling is going to change that. We have a nice long ride before we get where we are going for the night."

"The easy way for us is to just shoot you up with more drugs and have you sleep until we get where we are going. Or if you promise to behave yourself and not scream and yell, I will remove the tape from your mouth and move you from the floor to the much more comfortable seat. It is your choice. Are you going to behave yourself?"

I nodded, and the man reached down and in one hand lifted me up and put me in the van seat. Then he ripped the tape from my mouth, and it hurt like crazy.

I got a good look around the van and could see it is what my dad would call a panel van. The only windows were up front, and I was in a bench seat all the way in the back. If I remained in this seat there was no way I could signal anybody.

Luckily, I had watched lots of cop shows on TV with my dad and knew I would have to wait for my chance to escape. I had no idea how long I had slept after they drugged me, but I was sure my Mom and Dad, members of the police, and even the FBI would be hot on their trail.

Unfortunately for Kathy, not only was no one hot on their trail, there was no trail to get hot on. The kidnappers had planned this too well. This was not their first kidnapping; in fact, it was their sixth kidnapping this month and third one this week.

They had taken her from a rural location in Mississippi. The county was large and the county sheriff's department small. The kidnappers had taken her from a bus tour so even if her parents saw the kidnapping, they had no car to pursue. They were stuck traveling on a bus. The bus wouldn't pursue as that would mean putting other passengers at risk.

The child traffickers were at very little risk because they never held on to their hostages very long, usually less than 24 hours. They had a secure place to stash her until the phone call came telling them where to leave "the package". Each time the location was different. Sometimes it was an old barn or a vacant tobacco drying shed, other times it was a basement of some building.

Each time they delivered a package there would be an envelope full of cash and a new number to call with instructions on what to look for in the next delivery and a deadline. If there was any damage to the package it would be taken out of the next envelope.

They were pretty sure this was a bigger operation than just them because if for some reason they couldn't fill the requested order by the deadline, they were to call a number and report in. The person at the other end of the phone line would place another order for another package. There were probably half a dozen groups just like them because it seemed like the need for these special packages was endless.

Once they had the package and had made sure there was no pursuit, they called their mother and told her she would be getting a delivery and what time to expect it. Their mom handled it until they were given delivery instructions.

They never met the person or group they delivered to; Max called it a cutout. In the event the authorities caught one of them the only thing they could give up was the drop off destination which would never be used again.

CHAPTER 42

It took Snake's crew a few months to realize that the man in charge of the whole operation had chosen to use the slave's underground railroad from the civil war days to get packages from point A to point B.

Just like during the civil war, the home guard and slave hunters let over 100,000 slaves slip through their fingers. It was a fool proof plan, albeit 150 years old.

Back at the Blue Front Café, it was chaos. Kathy's parents missed her after about 10 minutes. She had told them she was going outside to get some pictures while they finished their meal. She had taken lots of pictures along the way. She said she was going to create a blog for other kids whose parents ripped them from where their roots were and moved them halfway across the country, just for a job.

They finished eating and went to round up Kathy. They went outside, and Kathy was nowhere to be found. They went out to the bus, no Kathy. They checked around the back of the Blue Front Café, no Kathy, Mrs. Sweet went back inside and checked the lady's room, no Kathy.

While her dad was walking across the parking lot he looked down and saw a red I phone exactly like the one they had given

Kathy. Mrs. Sweet came back outside to see if her husband had any luck, and saw the stricken look on her husband's face, and then she saw Kathy's cell phone in his hand.

"Oh my God! "she exclaimed.

Alerted by the screams outside his café, The owner went outside to see what the ruckus was all about. Hearing that Kathy probably was missing, he suggested she probably just wandered off. He was quick to change his mind when shown Kathy's dropped iPhone her dad had in his hand,

He then agreed, saying, "you are right, no girl kid that age leaves their cell phone behind voluntarily."

By now the other passengers began exiting the restaurant and realized something horrible must have happened.

One of the members of the VFW took charge when he heard what had happened. He had the tour guide call 911 and alert the sheriff's office that there had been a child abduction by the Blue Front Café. Another veteran wrote down a description of the clothing she was wearing and verified it with the other passengers.

The restaurant owner called both the state police and the Sheriff's office. He told them that both departments share the jurisdiction. It took the sheriff's deputy almost 45 minutes to get there as he was on the other side of the county. He hesitated to tell the parents, given the amount of lead time the kidnappers had the search area was already over 900 square miles.

Twenty minutes later Sergeant Larry Philips of the Alabama State Police showed up with a member of the Mississippi State Police, and two hours after that the FBI arrived and took charge.

Typically, the FBI doesn't respond to crimes in the state unless they are invited in except for bank robberies and kidnappings.

The FBI took the parents inside to get some background information.

CHAPTER 43

A quick examination of the parking lot showed no immediate clues to the kidnappers' possible identities. The parking lot was all crushed stone, so no tire tracks of the kidnapper's vehicle were available to make plaster casts.

The one piece of evidence they had was Kathy's cell phone, but because her dad had handled the phone it was unlikely there would be any useful fingerprints to match the kidnappers. The FBI still placed it in an evidence bag.

Sergeant Phillips wrote down the clothes she was wearing, got a picture of her from earlier that day that her mom had taken, and put out an all-points bulletin. He assured them that he had the state police issue an Amber Alert in a 4-state area. Mississippi, Louisiana, Tennessee, and his home state, Alabama.

Mr. & Mrs. Sweet just sat there in shock, wondering what could have happened to their little girl. Would they ever see her again? They knew all about child trafficking, they had watched a documentary on 60 Minutes about it. They had made the entire family watch it.

This happened to other people but not them. They told the FBI they weren't rich, they couldn't pay a ransom of thousands of dollars, what could they do? Maybe they could offer a reward of maybe 5 or 10 thousand dollars for her safe return no questions asked. They were willing to try anything to get their little girl back. They had to hope that the kidnappers would be swayed to accept their offer over what someone who wanted to keep her was willing to pay.

Kathy's parents provided the physical description of their daughter. They said that she should be able to be easily spotted because she had on a Kansas City Chiefs football jersey. After interviewing the parents and concluding that their daughter was not singled out but more likely a target of opportunity, he declared this was not just a kidnapping but more than likely a case of human trafficking.

The FBI had the sheriff's deputy drive Kathy's parents to their field office in Memphis. They had arranged a meeting with the press to get the word out about the kidnapped girl. What else could they do? The authorities didn't have a clue to go on.

CHAPTER 44

Kathy felt all alone but she tried to be strong and not cry. She kept trying to get clues that might help her later. Learning their names was no help because they called each other by nicknames. The one sitting with her on the back seat they called Snake. He had this ugly snake tattoo going up his arm under the short sleeve of his T-shirt only to emerge by his neck and look like it was about to strike.

The guy doing the driving they called Speedy he was short and really seemed jittery. Once when they pulled over so the men could relieve themselves, she watched Speedy take some pills and wash them down with a half empty bottle of whiskey. The last one they called Hoss. Sometimes they also called him Cartwright. He didn't say much and was larger than the other two men put together.

All three of them needed a shave and a bath. She had hoped when they stopped so the men could relieve themselves, she might get a chance to run away. She even told them she had to go but Snake promised if she could wait just a bit longer, they had planned for that possibility.

The men got in the van, and they drove about another hour before they pulled into a convenience store. There were no lights on and was obviously closed for the night. Snake cut the duct tape from her wrists and ankles then Hoss picked her up and carried her into the unlocked front door of the convenience store. He deposited her in front of the lady's restroom door and stationed himself at the door.

She went inside and a quick look around the dirty restroom and was disappointed to see there were no windows in the bathroom. She quickly did her business washed her hands in the dirty sink and used a paper towel to open the doorknob so she wouldn't have to touch it.

She left the restroom and Hoss escorted her to the soda machine and told her to get whatever flavor she wanted. Then they went to a back room where a fourth guy was cooking bacon and eggs. They talked while they ate but didn't really say anything that was of value except, they had to stash her at their mom's so they could go to their day job.

After that stop they drove for another couple of hours and then left the road and followed an old dirt track to an old barn. Hoss led the way to a big barn door and went inside the dark barn. Speedy shown his flashlight around the barn and laughed with glee as some rats were scared off by the flashlight's beam.

In the center of the barn was a post. Hanging from the post was a pair of shackles. Snake led her to a chair that was up against the pole and fastened a shackle tightly around each ankle. He gave a tug on the chain to make sure it was secure. He handed her a brown bag and told her there were a couple bacon and egg sandwiches and two bottles of water in it in case she got hungry or thirsty.

He shown his flashlight over in the corner and she saw what her dad called a chemical toilet and toilet paper.

Hoss told her that he wasn't going to tape her mouth shut tonight because if she yelled at the top of her lungs the only person who would hear her was their mom that lived next door and she was very mean. If she heard any yelling she would come out to the barn, give her a whipping, duct tape her wrists behind her back, and tape her mouth shut. Then Hoss said, "She had done that to other passengers that were here before you.

They left her a small battery powered lantern but told her if she left it on for a long period of time the batteries would run out and she would be left in total darkness.

They said they would be back tomorrow night to move her to the next station and they left. Once they had taken their flashlights with them the barn became pitch black. She quickly turned on the lantern and there was some comfort in the warm glow it gave off. She knew she should use the lantern sparingly but being alone in this dark barn scared her. With all she had been through today she was exhausted and found she needed to close her eyes for just a few minutes. She fell fast asleep.

CHAPTER 45

She awoke a few hours later to the hoot of a barn owl. She opened her eyes and for a moment she thought she was blind. Then she remembered she was chained up in an old barn. She reached around until her hands discovered the lantern and tried to turn it on only to realize the switch was on. She remembered she had it on when she had fallen asleep had the batteries run out while she slept? Had she wasted her only source of light in this horrible place? Tears began to fall from her eyes. She was unable to hold them back anymore. No need to put on a brave front to her kidnappers. Just when she thought things couldn't get any worse, she heard scurrying of the rats as they began to investigate the strange smells in their home. She heard a bag rustle and realized at least one of the rats had found the bacon sandwiches Snake had left for her. She couldn't help it, she screamed, again and again.

Ten minutes later she heard the barn door creak open and a lantern light showed a figure entering the barn. The glow of the lantern distorted the person's features. It wasn't until they were fully in the barn that Kathy could tell it was a woman. She was dressed in a long nightgown and carried a whip.

She demanded to know what the reason for the noise was in the middle of the night. Kathy told her about the rats and the bagged lunch and there being no light. The old woman stretched out her whip, Kathy tried to hide as much of herself as she could behind the pole when she heard the whip whistle through the air. Kathy felt sure she would feel the sting of the whip bite into her flesh. Again, the whip whistled and again she felt no pain. The old lady told her to get away from that pole, and again the whip snapped and again she had not been struck. It was then she realized the old woman's target wasn't her, but the rats. She told Kathy that she had told her boys many times not to bring food into the barn because it drives the rats crazy.

"Your boys," Kathy asked.

"Of course, they are my boys. I raised them mostly by myself. Their daddy was on the road much of the year. Running the fair, he is gone from March until snow flies. You'd best use the facilities while I have the light so you can see. When you are done, I'm headed back to bed, and I don't want to hear another peep coming from this barn. If I do, I can assure you this whip can discourage more than just rats. I prefer to not mark you up because you are worth a lot more to us if you aren't damaged goods."

Then she left and the darkness surrounded Kathy once again. Somehow in the middle of her prayer to be rescued Kathy fell asleep.

She awoke to a rooster crowing outside and with the rooster announcing the new day. Kathy could see there were enough cracks in the old wood siding that it let some of the gray light filter inside. Finally, she could start to see her surroundings.

She heard a chain rattle and in came the old woman from the night before, and she was carrying another sack. She tossed it to Kathy and told her she should eat it before the rats got wind of it. If she didn't eat it fast the rats would steal it like they did with her supper last night. Kathy looked in the bag and found two hot egg and sausage biscuits hot off the griddle, and two bottles of water.

She dug into the food like she hadn't eaten in days instead of the night before. Kathy thanked the woman for scaring the rats away with her whip the night before. The old woman said that she wasn't scaring them, just teaching them some manners and thinning the numbers out a little.

She then reached behind her and handed Kathy a stuffed animal and said that she tried telling Speedy that you were a little old for stuffed animals, but he wanted you to have it anyway. "I think Speedy kind of likes you." Just the thought of Speedy with his rotten teeth made her cringe.

Kathy asked how long she would be there, and the old woman said not to worry that her boys were close by and would be here every night to check up on her. She deposited four more water bottles and said that she would see her at lunch time. The barn door closed. The outside chain and lock were fastened. Again, she was alone. Alone to face the demons her mind could dream up. Fear of the unknown was very real.

CHAPTER 46

As promised that night the old lady's three sons came back to the farm. They brought Kathy cold corn dogs, some cotton candy, and some warm bottles of water to drink. The corn dogs tasted terrible, but she was so hungry she ate them anyway.

They told her that they were going to move her to her next destination the next night because their day job was moving locations. She also learned that the three had first spotted her at the Waffle House where she and her parents had eaten breakfast. They had overheard Kathy's families plans for the day and decided they would follow to see if an opportunity presented itself to take her. She learned that they had followed her parents' car until it went to the parking lot for the Blues tour. They watched her get off the tour bus and followed closely behind knowing they would eventually have a chance to nab her.

She knew that she might get a chance to escape when they were moving her. Limited by the length of chain, she searched everywhere in the barn that she could reach. She was unable to find anything she could use as a weapon.

During one of her searches, she had moved a bale of straw away from the barn wall and she had found an old piece of charcoal and etched in the barn wall was a list of eleven girls names. She carefully added her name to the bottom of the list before moving the bale of straw back in place.

The old lady brought her supper that night and commented that she had made the local news. She said that her parents must not care much for her because they had offered only $15,000.00 reward for her safe return. With that blonde hair of yours, we will get three times that for you on the open market. There are always a lot of people looking for little girls with nice long blonde hair like yours. Usually, we would cut your hair nice and short like a little boy before you left here, but we have found that even though it would help us disguise you it might cost us as much as $5,000.00 when we sell you to the next one up the line.

The old lady asked her if she had any idea how old the barn was?

When Kathy shook her head no, she told her that this very barn had been built before the civil war between the northern and southern states. It had been in her family all that time. Her ancestors had been southerners through and through, everyone except her great, great, Grandfather Jasper.

For some reason he was against slavery. In fact, this very barn was used to help slaves escape. It was part of the underground railroad. The Home Guard caught poor old Jasper helping the slaves escape. No trial, no being judged by his peers, just 20 feet of rope and a stout limb. They hung him in a cotton wood tree right next to the seven slaves they caught that same night right here in this barn. They burnt the house to the ground that night to send a message to anyone else who might get it in their mind to help runaway slaves. For some reason, they never did burn the barn. I have always wondered about that. Maybe one of the Home Guards that was here that night had plans for the barn, nobody knows for sure. Of course, I'm just guessing.

Kathy shivered at the thought of people being bought and sold and then being hung for wanting to live free or just helping someone to reach freedom.

She told me that her boys would be there to collect her around midnight, and I should make sure I used the bathroom before they took me because it was a long ride to the next station. There would be no pit stops between here and where they were taking me.

Kathy had just fallen asleep when she heard the barn door being unlocked. The three men entered the barn and undid the shackles. The skin on her ankles was rubbed raw by the shackles. Snake reached for a bottle on a shelf that had a rag stuck in the top. He tipped the bottle upside down and wet the rag with its contents. He told Hoss to hold her, and then he rubbed her scraped ankles with the wetted rag. Almost instantly it felt like her ankles were on fire. No matter how she kicked and fought she was unable to escape from Hoss's grip. Snake and Speedy just laughed. Snake said it was horse liniment and used to heal scrapes on horses' legs and it will heal those shackle scrapes on your legs in just a few days. Speedy laughed and told her that the horses didn't like it either.

She so wanted to run but Hoss was blocking the door while Snake taped her wrists behind her back. They led her out to the van and again placed her in the back seat next to Snake while Speedy drove and Hoss sat in the front passenger seat.

The three of them were talking about how stupid the people were that played the games of chance at the fair. Snake told of one guy that must have spent his entire paycheck trying to show off to his girlfriend what a great basketball player he was. He spent all that money and never did win a prize. His girlfriend got mad and left with another guy who had won a prize someplace else.

She now knew that the three of them and probably their father all worked at a carnival or a fair. Even their mother and father were in on the kidnapping. If she ever got away from them, she could tell that to the police. She also knew that their home was a farm that used to be on the underground railroad. All she needed to do now was escape.

CHAPTER 47

They drove through the night, the men taking turns driving. She hated it the most when Speedy was the one sitting next to her. He kept sliding over close to her and grinning with those rotted teeth of his. He looked so creepy. Once he ran his fingers through her hair and she choked back a scream. It was loud enough that Hoss slammed on the brakes. Snake took one look at Speedy and made him drive and Hoss replaced him sitting next to her. Of the three kidnappers Hoss seemed to be the nicest, but he was the quietest. Speedy and Snake looked mean and acted the same way.

She had no idea where they were, they didn't take any of the major highways which might have had big signs lit up by the van's headlights. Due to the late hour and the back roads, they were traveling, there were very few cars. All she had been able to learn from the way the men talked, was that their final destination was near Atlanta, Georgia, but that they had a stop before that. She knew with every minute that passed she was getting further and further away from her parents and deeper and deeper in trouble.

The steady sound of the vans tires on the pavement slowly lulled her to sleep. When she awoke the three kidnappers were drinking coffee poured from a thermos. It looked like they were eating some of those old corn dogs like they had brought her the night before. They offered her none and she asked for none even though her stomach seemed to want to join in on the corn dog feast.

When they finally pulled over alongside the road, she could see a mailbox lit by the headlights from the van. The men got out of the van and huddled together talking something over. She couldn't hear what they were saying, but she could tell they weren't very happy. While the three of them were out of the van this might be her only chance to escape. If she could just get in the driver's seat, she could put the van in gear, step on the gas and maybe even run them over.

Although her hands were taped together, and her ankles were immobilized by several layers of duct tape she thought she could make it to the driver's seat. She was forced to take baby steps because of the way her ankles were taped. Slowly she made her way to the back of the driver's seat. She was just about to slide in the seat when Snake opened the driver's door and said, "Just where do you think you might be going little lady?"

Kathy said the first thing that came into her mind. She told Snake that she needed to go to the bathroom. Snake lifted her out of the van and told Hoss to take her behind the tree and let her go to the bathroom. Before cutting the tape around her ankles so she could go, he tied a rope around her neck so she couldn't run.

While she was behind the tree, Snake seemed to make up his mind. From a few words said between the brothers she was then able to piece together what the issue was. It seems that they were supposed to put her in a hidden room in this old house which was supposed to be abandoned. Only now, based on the lights burning in the windows, a car in the driveway, and a sold sign in the front yard the house was no longer abandoned.

The problem the brothers were faced with was this was the drop off location. They had used it before; this is where they had been directed to leave the package. Waiting for them inside would be an envelope containing $20,000 dollars. If they failed to deliver the package, they couldn't take the money. If they didn't take the money their mom would use her bull whip on the three of them. They had no way to contact anyone to alert them that the house was no longer empty. If they failed to leave the package where they were told to leave it there would be no pay day. No $10,000 divided evenly between the boys after their mom took her share, $10,000. None of them was willing to go back and tell their mom that they had failed to follow the delivery instructions so she wouldn't be able to collect her $10,000 dollar fee. They had all felt the end of her bull whip before.

CHAPTER 48

The boys knew where they were supposed to leave her was in a secret room. The likelihood that someone just moving into the house would have discovered the hidden room was very unlikely. Finally, they decided to go ahead with the plan. They put tape on her mouth and then wound it around the back of her head, so it was secure. They taped her legs so tightly she couldn't move an inch. They then completely wrapped her body in duct tape, so she resembled a mummy, and carried her to the path by the front porch.

They bound her so tightly she couldn't possibly move or make a sound. The men crawled under the porch between the two hedges, dragged her to the crawl space under the house. Snake held the flashlight while Hoss pulled open the trap door. Hoss lifted her up and just kind of tossed her in the room. Speedy followed her in there and she could hear Snake tell him to just grab the envelope and get out of there. They put the floor panel in place and Kathy was plunged in total darkness. At first, she panicked having no idea where she was, or if she had been left to die.

Then she thought about the times she had spent in Sunday school and the many lessons she had been taught. The Jesus she had learned about would never leave her, so she really wasn't alone. She thought of her situation and realized there were some things to be thankful for. She was warm and dry, no matter where she was, this was a better place than that old barn with the rats running around. She started to pray as she had been taught. "<u>Our Father, who art in heaven Hallowed be thy name.</u>"

She then remembered the story about Jonah and the whale, he was in a worse situation than she was. God rescued him.

Even though she couldn't see a single thing she decided she would roll and see if she could figure out how big the room she had been left in was. At first, hesitantly, she rolled to the left and then to the right. Feeling no boundaries, she increased the distance she rolled each time until she finally rolled into a wall. Luckily there were so many layers of duct tape on her it cushioned the blow. Then she had another thought, maybe if she rotated her body around, she could get her feet next to the wall, bend her knees a little bit and kick both legs against the wall. It took her a good 10 minutes to get in the desired position and she began kicking the wall. It gave a nice hollow noise. Every few minutes she would give it another try.

PART III

CHAPTER 49

Dr. Lee first fixed her dogs some supper and then fixed supper for herself. She always questioned if she was doing it in the right order because whichever way she did it the dogs seemed to take it personally. On one hand if she didn't give them their dinner precisely at 5:00 they would sit there and stare at her as if she had forgotten how to tell time. If she fed them precisely at 5:00 they were done eating by 5:01. She was convinced that neither dog ate their food. They typically inhaled it. As if by magic, once she told them it was okay to eat their food, they acted like they hadn't eaten in a month.

Once she fed them, she prepared her own dinner. During the preparation time they stared at her, praying that she would drop some tiny morsel on the floor so they wouldn't starve to death before morning. When she tried to eat her dinner, they decided it was time to sit in her lap. Her lap was not made for two full grown labs. There probably wasn't a lap made big enough to hold two full grown labs. They watched her eat everything on her plate, their eyes following every movement of the fork from her plate to her mouth. If she fixed her meal before feeding them, they would sit there and cry as if she had violated every pet rule in the world.

Tonight, something was different. The dogs wolfed down their food just like normal but when she brought her food in the living room to watch TV, they weren't paying any attention to her at all. They were sniffing around the secret passage wall to the hidden room. At one point the dogs alerted and sounded off with a deep bark. They had never done that before.

Her husband wouldn't be home for two more days, so she phoned Mr. Cristman. "Le Roy" she said, "this is Dr. Lee."

"What can I do for you Doc.?"

"I hate to ask you a favor and please apologize to your wife for me, but would you mind coming back over and nailing that trap door in place. The dogs are acting funny and are sniffing at the bottom of the hidden wall. I am afraid we didn't get that trap door properly in place and I must have a critter in there."

"No problem, Doc. Let me grab my grandsons and we will be right over. They probably did a poor job putting that trap door on. We will fix it."

Ten minutes later we pulled in the Dr.'s driveway and again we were greeted by her Labrador greeting committee. The Dr. met us on the front porch, and we entered the house. She led us to the living room, and I noticed all the living room lights were turned on and all the furniture that could be moved had been moved in front of the hidden wall. As added protection she was carrying a super soaker squirt gun. I couldn't help but laugh.

She saw my questioning look and said while she was waiting for me to arrive, she did a search on raccoons on the internet. She had learned that some are rabid and rabid animals are scared of light and water.

That explained the living room remodel and her weapon of choice. I couldn't help but chuckle even more.

Dr. Lee said, "You can laugh if you want. This is one woman who isn't afraid to protect herself."

CHAPTER 50

"Right before I called, I started hearing thumping," she said.

"Thumping I questioned." "In all my 66 years I have never heard a raccoon thump. This is getting very interesting."

"Well, it's thumping," she said.

She handed me the flashlight and I told the boys to slide the panel back just as soon as I entered the hidden room in case the "Wild Raccoon" charges.

Dr. Lee said, "Le Roy, you be careful in there. Don't you get bitten by a rabid raccoon."

She even tried to offer me her super soaker which I declined.

I entered the room; the boys slid the panel back and shined my flashlight on the floor and could see the panel the boys had dug out earlier. it was in place and secure. No raccoon, rabid or otherwise got in here that way. As I played the light beam along the floor I heard a thump, it was definitely a thump just like Doc had said. The light neared the sound of the thump, and all curled up in a ball was, I wasn't sure what it was. Then I saw a bright red sneaker with a foot in it.

I quickly realized it was a child. I knelt beside it, and I could hear a muffled scream. "I called Doc to come in here." I was afraid I might scare the child to death if I was to pick it up. I knew Doc would have a much better idea how to treat this traumatized child than I would. A closer examination revealed that someone must have used two rolls of duct tape to bind up this little girl. Doc started whispering to the little girl trying to reassure her that she was safe, that we wouldn't let anyone hurt her. Doc laid down on the floor by the little girl and asked her if she could give her a hug. The little girl nodded hesitantly. Doc gently put her arm around the girl and gave her a small hug.

Doc asked the girl, "how about we get you out of this dark room and into a lighted room and get this duct tape off.

I hollered to my grandsons to open the sliding wall and carried the girl out. As Doc carefully started unwinding the tape both Duke and Duchess thought this was a new kind of game and were overly willing to help remove the duct tape. If it weren't for the somber occasion, it would have been funny.

"While you are seeing to this little girl, I am going to call the Sheriff." It was 8:00 at night and I knew that the Sheriff, Burt Kaper would be home unless he was working late on a case. After I told him what we found, he would be working very late tonight. I knew Burt from working with him a few years ago while he put together a search and rescue team to find two kids who had wandered away from their parent's campsite. Due to the search pattern, he had dictated and the fast response from the people in town, the kids were found in less than an hour. The kids had seen what they thought was a dog but was really a mother coyote taking dinner back to her pups in the den. That could have ended a lot different and badly.

CHAPTER 51

I spoke to Burt, and he said he would be there in 20 minutes. In the meantime, he was sending a deputy that could be here in under 10.

I told the boys what was going on and sent them to my toolbox to grab a pair of scissors, the bottle of Goo-be- gone, and I wanted one of them to give me their shirt. I took Harry's shirt and went back in the room with Doc and the little girl. The boys brought the requested items back in and I told them to grab a lamp from the living room to put it in this room and then wait on the porch for the deputy sheriff to arrive and guide him back here.

Doc was trying hard to get the tape off but there was so much of it, and it was stuck to her like iron bars. I told the little girl we were going to remove the tape from her eyes first. That I needed her to keep her eyes shut because I was going use a liquid that might smell a little funny, but it will make the tape let go of your skin and it won't hurt when I pull it off. The girl nodded and shook at the same time.

I was concerned the little girl would go into shock. From the look in Doc's eyes, I could tell she was thinking along the same lines

Doc held her while I put some Goo-b-gone on my handkerchief and gently soaked the duct tape, they had put over her eyes. Just as advertised the Goo-b-gone dissolved the adhesive on the tape and the tape covering the little girls' eyes loosened right up and I was able to remove that piece covering her eyes. She gave me a look and grabbed onto Doc like her life depended on it. We did the same thing to remove the tape stuck to her lips. It too came off without a hitch.

She was taking in big gulps of air, almost hyper-ventilating. When she got her breath back, I told her we had to cut her football jersey off because there was so much tape holding it to her that she would be graduating from college by the time we got all that adhesive off. With that she started to cry. She said it was her favorite team and her favorite player Patrick Mahomes from the Kansas City Chiefs. I promised her I would replace her jersey with a brand new one. While Doc used the scissors to remove the jersey, I handed her my grandsons' shirt and went out to talk to the deputy.

I had the deputy call for an ambulance. I sent Shane to go grab a blanket from one of the beds and bring it to me. I called into Doc to make sure the coast was clear and brought in the blanket Shane had brought me. I was pretty sure that after everything this little girl had been through, she was going to go into shock if she wasn't there already. I called the Missus, told her what was going on and she said she would be right over.

Sheriff Burt arrived, and I gave him an update. He said he had been on the phone with child protective services, They were sending a case worker over. Just then the ambulance showed up and the Sheriff told them too standby.

Moments later Doc came out holding the little girl in her arms and said, "Everybody this is Kathy. Kathy this is everybody." I thought I saw a little smile turn up at that introduction. She was hanging on Doc like there was no tomorrow.

Judy came in and headed straight to the kitchen, she had brought some of her famous chicken noodle soup and started heating it on the stove.

Kathy had not yet told us her full name or where she was from, she had been unable to tell us who her parents were or where she was taken. I thought it was surprising that the ones she connected with besides Doc was my two grandsons. Each one sat on either side of Doc while Kathy sat in Doc's lap covered up by the blanket. My wife placed a steaming bowl of chicken noodle soup in front of her, but she refused to touch it. She looked at both boys and my wife picked up on it and dished up a bowl of soup for each of the boys and when they started eating so did, Kathy.

CHAPTER 52

Doc observed and said, "right now it is a trust thing. She trusts me and she trusts the two boys. The rest of the adults not yet. She has trust issues with adults right now, and maybe for a long time to come."

The chicken noodle soup turned out to have some magic qualities since after eating it the little girl wasn't shaking beneath the blanket as much. It may have prevented her from going into shock.

The sheriff and I went into the dining room to talk. The sheriff asked if we had any idea how long the girl had been in there. I told the sheriff that it had to have been this evening, probably right after dark. I explained how the boys had been in the room earlier today. How they had discovered the trap door in the floor. How they had removed it and showed it to me. I told him it wasn't original and the date on the handle.

The dogs had alerted at around 8:00 so that was probably going to be the closest approximation of the time. No telling how long she had been in captivity or what she had gone through.

The sheriff wanted to know how long I had known the Dr. and what did I know about her.

"Tell me you don't think she had anything to do with this. She can't possibly be a suspect."

The Sheriff said, "Le Roy you know how this thing works, everyone is a suspect until they aren't. The law enforcement team may seem like it moves slowly. At times you are right, but by following the proven path we are more than likely not going to miss anything. We will have a case the district attorney can take to court and put the bad guys behind bars where they belong. So, tell me how you know the good Dr."

"I met Dr. Lee about three years ago at the VA medical center. I had volunteered to serve on a team looking into reducing the number of veteran suicides, which currently stands at 22 a day. Dr. Lee volunteers her time, she is a highly respected psychologist who brought a lot to the team. During our time on the committee, we found we shared the love of Labrador retrievers, gardening, and a love of history. We became good friends, and we trade her chickens' eggs for my fruits and vegetables. That's why we were here this morning. While we were here, she showed my grandsons and me the secret room that her husband had found. That they thought might have been used as part of the underground railroad."

I told him about the trap door the boys had found, and they may want to dust it for prints because that trap door had to be the way they got the girl in there. "You will want my prints and my grandsons prints to rule them out."

"The boy's prints will be easy enough to rule out just because of the size, and I can get your prints from the time you were in the Navy," the Sheriff said.

Just then the woman from child protective services showed up. She attempted to take the little girl from Dr. Lee, but she just hung on Dr. Lee's neck that much harder. She began to cry again. The woman backed off and Dr. Lee calmed her down again.

The Sheriff took charge and told the agent from the child protective services that at least for tonight the girl would be staying in the very comfortable arms of Dr. Lee.

Dr. Lee explained she was going to take the girl in the bedroom for privacy and give her a quick once over to see if there were any obvious medical issues that needed immediate medical attention. In about 15 minutes she returned, still with the girl's arms tightly wound around her neck.

She said, "barring a closer examination by a medical Doctor it would appear except for some torn skin around her ankles and some bruising of her forearms and legs physically she is going to be fine. Mentally, it is too soon to tell, what she needs more than anything is a good night's sleep. But after everything she has been through is going to be extremely difficult."

CHAPTER 53

"I suggest that she stay with me tonight and we will see how things look in the morning."

The Sheriff nodded in agreement, dispatched the ambulance back to the hospital and suggested the child protective agent meet them back here at 10 AM in the morning.

The sheriff said, he would start setting up roadblocks on the major roads out of the county. He said the person or persons that did this are more than likely long gone, but they should turn over every stone and they might just get lucky.

He asked if I could possibly stay there tonight because that would free up his deputy to assist in setting up roadblocks.

The sheriff was almost right. The three brothers were now safely out of the county but hadn't left until they had witnessed the arrival of the deputy. and that was how they knew their $15,000 was gone for good. They would be expected to pay back that $15,000 or find a suitable replacement and find one fast. They now needed to wait for a phone call to tell them what actions to take. The girl had seen all their faces and could identify all three of them. Snake knew what action he wanted to take. His desired actions would be protecting the three of them.

Before leaving the sheriff said, "Le Roy, I know you have a concealed carry permit are you armed and willing to protect that little girl?"

"I am, and I am," I replied. "I even have a super soaker squirt gun in case any rabid raccoon's show up." He looked at me with questions on his lips. "I'll explain it all tomorrow."

Judy packed up the boys to take them home and put them to bed. They pleaded that they wanted to camp out with me in the living room, but the subject was not up for debate.

Dr. Lee had taken the little girl in her bedroom and was planning on holding her throughout the night to help her battle the nightmares she would be having. I took the two labs, Duchess and Duke with me and we checked the security of the house making sure all the doors and windows were shut and locked. We went out on the porch and the two dogs ran out in the yard and did their business.

We locked the front door went into the living room where I had every intention of stretching out on the couch only to see that Duke and Duchess had beaten me to it. Each of them was stretched out on an end of the couch leaving no room for me. I jokingly told them, that's okay I wanted the recliner anyway.

I knew that the Duke and Duchess would alert me if anyone decided to sneak in the house. I closed my eyes and sleep soon overtook me.

CHAPTER 54

When I awoke the sky was just turning gray. I went to the front door followed closely by my two sleeping companions. I let them out and they did an outside sniff around. They both chose a spot to decorate the lawn and then bounded up the stairs to greet me. Both dogs gave me the stare, and I knew what that meant, I was expected to provide their breakfast and they preferred I did that five minutes ago. Not knowing where Dr. Lee kept the dog's food, I told them that. The dogs walked over and sat down on the floor in front of a tall cabinet. I opened it and right there in a tightly closed tub was the object of their interest. I opened the tub and then glanced around the kitchen for their food bowls and spotted them in a corner. Each one had their names on them. The pink one was for the Duchess and the blue for the Duke. I fed them and gave them fresh water. After they finished eating and had a healthy long gulp from the water bowl, they went to the door leading to Dr. Lee's bedroom and lay down.

I spent the next half hour thinking about everything that had taken place here in the past 24 hours. Last night a brief visit by the crime scene crew arrived and had used yellow police boundary tape to rope off the area that would need to be searched more thoroughly.

Crime scene tape was sealing off the hidden room and the path out front between the two hedges.

Today, Doc's place would be a madhouse with all the state forensic people coming and going. Detectives from the state would be here, not to mention every news truck within a four-state area would be arriving to cover the biggest national news story in weeks.

Time to call my wife with my next brainstorm. I told Judy what was taking place here and she immediately came to the same conclusion I did. Bring Kathy over to our house and get her away from all that activity and noise.

Just then I heard three vehicles coming up the driveway. Duke and Duchess heard them too and barked announcing the new arrivals. It was Burt the Sheriff, a state police van that had a sign identifying it as the Alabama State Crime Scene Department, and a state police officer and car.

The sheriff and the state police sergeant got out of their cars as did three crime scene technicians. I opened the door before Duke and Duchess knocked it down and went out to greet everyone and welcome them. Everyone stooped down to give the dogs a friendly scratch behind the ears or the belly except Sergeant Phillips of the state police. He almost kicked at the dogs when they drew near looking to make friends with the new arrival. When I saw this, I called the dogs back to the house, and they bounded up the steps.

I wondered what was wrong with that guy. Maybe he just didn't like dogs or had a bad experience when he was a kid. It was just strange, any law enforcement officer I had ever met had liked dogs, if they didn't like dogs, they never tried to kick one.

CHAPTER 55

Sergeant Phillips briefed the crime scene technicians. He said he wanted to be first to see any potential evidence the crime scene technicians uncovered.

The crime scene techs started by examining the hedges looking for any threads of clothing that may have gotten snagged while the kidnappers had passed through it the night before. There was too much pine straw around the bottom of the hedges for them to get any plaster casts of footprints. They removed the trap door, placed it in a large evidence bag and then went inside the hidden room to look and see if there was any chance there was something that might provide them with clues as to who did this.

They said that they were going to need to take the little girls clothing because it too was evidence.

As if it were planned, Judy and the boys showed up carrying three Walmart shopping bags. Unless I missed my guess there would be new clothes in those bags. Judy had overheard the request by the crime scene technicians and went to Dr. Lee's door and knocked softly. Dr. Lee explained that the little girl's first name was Kathy, who was currently in Dr. Lee's big antique claw foot bathtub soaking in her favorite bubble bath. Together they bundled up the old clothes, Judy took them out to the technicians. Dr. Lee laid out three different outfits for Kathy to choose from when she exited the bath.

Dr. Lee had given her a new toothbrush last night and while she brushed her teeth Dr. Lee ran a comb through her damp hair.

Despite all she had been through, she slept pretty soundly only waking a few times and once realizing she was safe in Dr. Lee's big old feather bed and in her protective arms, she drifted back off to sleep.

The sleep, bath, and new clothes had done wonders for Kathy. Gone were the deep circles under her red eyes caused by too many days of terror and lack of sleep. The dogs came over to greet her when they came out of the bedroom. Their tails were going a mile a minute as they took turns licking Kathy's previously tear streaked cheeks. The dogs even got a little giggle from Kathy, a sure sign she was starting to let go of some of the trauma she had been put through. She still stayed almost glued to the Dr's side.

When Dr. Lee asked her if she was hungry Kathy nodded in agreement. The grandsons seconded that idea. Dr. Lee suggested I take the boys out to the chicken coop and gather up some fresh eggs while she, Kathy, and Judy whipped up a batch of biscuits and start the bacon frying. At the word bacon both dogs' ears perked up, they obviously were used to sharing the bacon at the breakfast table.

The boys and I headed out to the chicken coop with baskets in hand to gather any eggs the chickens had laid since yesterday. afternoon.

Neither one of my grandsons had ever collected eggs before so it should be quite a learning experience. Dr. Lee had eight chickens that were laying eggs. The chickens had been given straw to make their nests. I showed the boys how to search the empty nests for any eggs and each one collected several. I told them that they needed to inspect each egg and make sure there were no cracks in any of them. Any cracked eggs we would have to toss them out. The boys collected the eggs from the vacant nests but the last two had hens sitting on their eggs.

The boys asked how we got the hens off their nests so they could check for eggs. I reached my hand over to the first chicken and received a peck on the back of my hand for my trouble. I looked around the chicken coop and spotted just what I was looking for, a small shovel. I used the shovel to gently lift the chicken off her nest and then with my other hand I took out the eggs.

The boys followed my example and got the eggs from under the other sitting chicken. They wanted to know how often to collect the eggs. I told them at least twice in the morning and sometimes a third time in late afternoon.

I inspected the nests, and they were still clean and could go a few more days before replacing the straw. We went to the house and the boys were proud to show off the dozen eggs they had collected.

The boys asked Dr. Lee where to put the eggs and she showed them her egg refrigerator. It was in the basement. She stressed to them that she always put the freshest eggs in the back. This was called FIFO. She said it stood for First In First Out.

She grabbed two dozen eggs from the front of the stack and carried them to the kitchen counter. She whipped up a batch of scrambled eggs to go with the bacon my wife was frying and the biscuits that had just come out of the oven.

Everyone enjoyed the hearty breakfast, I for one should not have eaten that third biscuit.

CHAPTER 56

After breakfast Dr. Lee took Kathy and my two grandsons into her study to have a chat. While she was in her study she phoned a judge that she knew, explained what was going on with Kathy and was granted an emergency custody order to keep her in the Doctor's capable hands.

While they were in the study the Sheriff shared the news that they believed they have found the parents. They put a picture of Kathy over the law enforcement network, and got an immediate response from a couple in Memphis. Their daughter had been kidnapped 11 days ago. The authorities are 95% sure was a match. The parents were able to identify the clothing she had been wearing and even the name was a match. "They are Mr. & Mrs. Sweet and are in the process of moving from Phoenix, Arizona to, of all places Prattville, Alabama. Le Roy, looks like you will have some new neighbors in the next couple of weeks. The parents are being driven here now by the Mississippi State Police and their car by a deputy. They will be met at the state line by the Alabama State Police and brought here along with the Sweets car.

Upon their arrival we will delay the family reunion until we are sure the parents had nothing to do with the abduction. The only way we can do that is if Kathy starts talking."

I said, "I'm sure that is what Dr. Lee is trying to do right now.

The sergeant from the state police said it was procedure that in cases of kidnapping the FBI be called in. The FBI had been working the case from the Memphis field office and would be arriving in about an hour.

Just then the study door opened, and Dr. Lee came out holding Kathy by the hand and she introduced her as Kathy Sweet. She wants to see her parents and she said when she was taken, they were in Mississippi at some place called the Blue Front café.

All the law enforcement tried asking Kathy questions and she hid behind Dr. Lee her protector.

Dr. Lee said, "that is NOT the way we are going to treat this little girl. You may write the questions you would like answered in the order you want them answered when she is comfortable talking about it, we will try and answer your questions. The key words here are when she is comfortable talking about it. As of right now she appears to be comfortable with the boys and myself. Don't any of you attempt to force this issue. I have already contacted the judge; a personal friend of mine, and he has temporarily put her in my care."

The state police sergeant looked upset, but the sheriff spoke up and said, "if that was my daughter, I would want Dr. Lee doing what was best for my child and you would too."

Grudgingly the state policeman nodded his head in agreement. "When would she be able to answer our questions, he wanted to know."

Dr. Lee said, "it might be as early as tomorrow, might not be until a couple of weeks from now. That little girl has been through a horrible experience. Asking her to remember every little detail and make her go through it again is criminal. What she needs right now is normalcy so she can put this behind her like a bad dream. She did share with me that she was not sexually assaulted because the men said she would be worth a lot more if she was untouched. We still need to have her examined by a medical professional, I have contacted a neighbor who is a female nurse practitioner and will be here in about 15 minutes.

If you need something to chew on there are plenty of biscuits and hot coffee to wash them down."

Those pushing for details about the kidnappers looked sheepishly at one another. This Dr. Lee was like a mother tiger protecting her young.

CHAPTER 57

The boys needed something to do so I took them back to the chicken coop and we fed the chickens. It seems like Duke and Duchess had become bored with the activity in the house and because no one was sharing their biscuits or bacon they decided to tag along. While the chickens left their nests to peck at the breakfast the boys had provided, I took the opportunity to teach them how to clean out the old nesting material and replace it with new.

I jokingly told the boys they would make good chicken farmers one day; we all had a good laugh.

The boys wanted to know what was going to happen to Kathy and I told them her parents were on their way here, once they got here, they would be making many of those decisions for her. We talked about what a horrible summer vacation she had so far. I agreed. The boys shared with me that when they were in the study with the Dr. and Kathy that she couldn't remember anything that happened to her before we found her all taped up in that room. Kathy can't answer all those questions they keep asking her. How can that be?

I told them, "that her mind was trying to protect her. When some people experience horrible events in their lives, like Kathy being kidnapped, the mind kind of erases those memories and the pain that it caused. What Dr. Lee is trying to do is bring those memories back to the surface in a controlled and safe manner, so she doesn't have to deal with the pain those memories are likely to cause."

Duke and Duchess brought us a tennis ball and it was obvious they thought it was play time. The boys took turns tossing the tennis ball for the dogs to retrieve. I looked at them and realized that 10 years old was the perfect age to be a boy. Not a care in the world, amused by the simple things life has to offer, and they still think of their grandfather as a superhero.

Soon the dog's tongues were hanging out of their mouths from retrieving the tennis ball. We walked back to the house the dogs gulped down the water from their water bowls. Without being asked the boys refilled the bowls.

CHAPTER 58

The nurse practitioner had finished her examination of Kathy. Except for the marks on her ankles from when she had been shackled, she gave her a clean bill of physical health. Her prescription for Kathy was to go have some fun while in a safe environment.

Just then Kathy's parents arrived, and they had a family reunion. The state police and the sheriff watched the exchange between parents and daughter and immediately ruled out any parental involvement in the kidnapping. Kathy introduced Shane and Harry to her parents and said they were like her brothers only nicer. Both boys blushed at being told they were nice.

The parents wanted to know what happens next. The Sheriff spoke up and said that Kathy had information that was critical to the investigation but still might be in danger from the kidnappers which puts her at risk. She would need round the clock protection at least for a while.

Kathy's dad spoke up, "I am supposed to be finding a house to buy and move my family before the end of the month."

Next Dr. Lee spoke up and said, "not to forget Kathy is going to need some help from me, or someone of your choosing, like me, to help her recover from this nightmare."

Kathy's dad spoke up and told Dr. Lee, they would greatly appreciate it if she would continue working with their daughter.

Dr. Lee said, "I will be happy to continue working with Kathy."

"The nurse said she needed to have some kid fun too," Harry added.

Judy spoke up, "that settles it." All eyes shifted to her. "Mr. & Mrs. Sweet you and your daughter are moving in with us. Kathy will be in good hands with us while you go house hunting, Le Roy is more than capable of protecting her. The boys can see to it that she has fun like going swimming in our pool. Even Abby our dog will help Kathy get her life back."

The room was silent for a minute and then the Sheriff spoke up, "That works for us with a couple slight modifications. I will have my patrol deputy make extra passes in front of your place and Le Roy; I am going to have to deputize you."

"Fine by me," I said.

My grandsons' eyes got as big as saucers when the sheriff handed me a badge and said, "I now deputize you in accordance with the law of Autauga County in the great state of Alabama." The state police said that they also would increase the patrols in the area.

The FBI arrived on the scene spoke with the Sheriff, nodded their heads in agreement, and as quickly as they arrived on the scene they left.

A small caravan left Dr. Lee's home and drove the short distance to mine with the Sheriff leading the way. Upon arrival, Judy showed the Sweets to their rooms. She said at least for now they would move a single bed in with them so Kathy would feel safe and in case she awoke in the middle of the night with any bad dreams.

Mrs. Sweet said, "don't bother there is plenty of room in that king sized bed for the three of us. I don't think I will ever let her out of my sight ever again."

Judy said, "I completely understand."

I made a quick phone call to coach Hilgendorf, he said he would be happy to grant me the favor I had asked of him.

Since the Sweets hadn't made any plans with any realtor, I phoned my realtor friend Paul Harper. I told him everything that had happened to this family, and he said that he would meet with them at 1:00 that afternoon at our home.

Kathy's parents had a private discussion. Because her mom was not willing to be separated from her daughter for even an instant they decided that her husband would look at houses with the realtor while she stayed close at hand with Kathy.

The boys asked if they could take Kathy with them to pick the vegetables from the garden. I saw that inclusion the boys were offering to Kathy was a step in the direction of normalcy. I told them to ask Kathy's mother.

CHAPTER 59

Kathy's mother looked at me with fear filled eyes until I told her I would be in the garden as well. She gave a hesitant nod signaling okay. All three kids took off towards the shed to grab their baskets and then to the garden. I grabbed my hoe and did some weeding a few rows over from where the kids were picking beans. The boys were teaching Kathy the tricks they had learned. She was a quick learner.

The boys were asking what on the outside might have been innocent questions but in fact was slowly dragging Kathy out of her protective shell one vegetable at a time. The boys said they had never eaten at a restaurant called the Blue Front Café and Kathy was able to describe it. When Kathy admitted to having eaten a cheeseburger the boys remembered it was time for lunch.

It's a little bit early for lunch so why don't you first rinse the vegetables off like I showed you and then ask Kathy's mom if Kathy can go swimming in the pool with you. The three of them took off like they had rockets in their pockets. I followed them up to the house and saw them doing as requested and then laying out the vegetables to dry.

They told their grandmother that the vegetables and fruits they had picked that morning were staged on the table on the porch so she could choose what ones she needed for supper that evening.

Kathy asked her mom if she could join the boys in the pool while they made lunch for the kids.

Again, Mrs. Sweet glanced my way looking for my approval I said, "only one question, can she swim?"

"Can she swim?" her mother asked. "Sometimes I think she is part fish. She swam at the Y back home and has been on the juniors' swim team for the past two years."

She went upstairs with Kathy while she changed into her bathing suit. I went out on the deck and watched three kids splashing in the pool as if none of them had a care in the world.

Lunch was served and surprisingly the boys each had a small salad to go along with their baloney sandwiches. I think the salad was eaten because Kathy ate a salad for lunch. It always amazed me how a woman, any woman, can change the way a guy thinks.

During lunch Dr. Lee called and wanted to have another one-on-one therapy session with Kathy this afternoon.

The boys and I set up the fruit and vegetable stand for the afternoon sales. When Kathy was done with her therapy session she and her mother came out to our makeshift fruit and vegetable stand and pitched right in with the sales.

I asked Mrs. Sweet how the therapy session went, and she said, "Dr. Lee was impressed by how much the boys had made her part of their group. She did mention that if we could start getting her some interaction with your adult friends and neighbors, it might help her deal with what happened with her."

After we closed the stand down for the evening the three of them counted out the money they had made. Instead of putting it in two stacks like they had done before they made three stacks this time, giving one to Kathy.

The boys and I took the baskets back to the shed and they said that they had something they needed to ask me. With today's profits from the stand both boys had nearly $500.00 dollars in their bank accounts. They told me that they had talked it over and wanted to make Kathy a full partner in their vegetable and fruit sales including the profits before she got there. "But we don't know how to do that."

I was extremely moved by what the boys had decided to do. I asked them why they wanted to do that, and they told me it was because it was the right thing to do. I love those boys; they catch on quick.

CHAPTER 60

That night, after the kids went to bed Mr. Sweet showed his wife the properties, they had looked at that day and explained the pluses and minuses of each one. Paul Harper had six more he thought they should look at before they started to decide. He also suggested that Mr. Sweet pick out his top three favorites and then he could stay home with Kathy and Paul would have his associate Debbie Whitehouse take his wife to those three. Hopefully she would choose 1 of the 3. "Having Debbie show the houses to your wife brings a woman's perspective that neither you nor I possess." He said, "95% of the time the decision on which house to buy ultimately comes down to the wife.

"That sounds like a plan," the Sweet's agreed.

"The boys and I have a little business to do at the bank in the morning," I said. "They really would like Mrs. Sweet and Kathy to join us. Kathy will have an opportunity to meet another adult friend of mine that works at the bank."

"That sounds okay," Mrs. Sweet responded.

"I really need to go to Walmart and get Kathy a new bathing suit she is growing out of that one. How do you think we should pull that off and keep her safe," she asked?

"The boys and I will keep Kathy company in the truck in the parking lot while you go inside to get her a new suit."

Mrs. Sweet said, "that sounds perfect."

The five of us all entered the bank and saw that Carol was with another customer, so we waited for a few minutes until she was free.

She came over and said, "how are my little depositor friends today?"

The boys replied, "just fine Miss Carol."

She said, "are you here to make another deposit from your fruit and vegetable stand?"

"Kinda sort of," Harry said.

"Our friend Kathy needs to open an account too," Shane replied.

"We can certainly do that," Carol said, "it will only take a few minutes." There was some paperwork for Mrs. Sweet to sign and then Kathy had her own account with $119.00. Kathy couldn't believe the boys were giving her a full share of the fruits and vegetable sales the previous day.

The boys then asked Carol if they could speak to her in private. She led them to her desk, and they told her what they wanted to do with the money in their accounts. Carol looked at me and I nodded my agreement. She brought some paperwork for me to sign, and then collected all the children's savings books, went to a teller window and returned about 5 minutes later. Le Roy those are some amazing grandsons you have there. I nodded in agreement. Kathy looked at her savings book again only to find the amount was no longer $119.00 but $470.23.

"What, how, where did all that money come from, she asked?"

Shane said, "Harry and I talked it over and decided to make you a full partner of our fruit and vegetable business."

"I didn't start until yesterday," Kathy replied

Harry's response was, "You would've, if you could've."

Shane said, "think of it as you were on emergency leave."

Mrs. Sweet looked at me and I shrugged my shoulders and said, "it was their idea."

Mrs. Sweet leaned down and gave both boys a kiss on the cheek. "Thank you, thank you for being such good friends to Kathy."

Both boys' faces turned red from embarrassment, their faces turned even redder when Kathy gave them each a kiss too. Mrs. Sweet asked the boys why they did that, and she got the same answer from both. We did it because it was the right thing to do.

Well, I said, "next stop Walmart."

The local Walmart was always jam packed. It didn't seem to matter what time of the day or night. I got a parking spot about 10 rows from the front. Mrs. Sweet got out of the truck and entered the store. When she had been gone about 5 minutes a white van backed into a handicapped spot right near the front entrance. Three men climbed out of the van; Kathy's face turned white as a ghost. They entered Walmart.

"It's them," she said.

"Who?" the boys asked.

"The men who took me," she replied.

I asked her if she was sure, she said, "definitely. "See the one with the snake tattoo on his arm. The big one they call Hoss and the little one they call him speedy. It's the same men."

"Okay here is what we are going to do. Harry use my phone and call 911 tell them where we are and that their deputy is going to arrest three men accused of kidnapping," I said.

Shane, under the seat you are sitting on is a small toolbox. Open it and give me both bottles of super glue. Keep the doors locked and under no circumstances leave the truck. You boys stay here and watch over Kathy.

CHAPTER 61

As soon as I had the super glue in hand and heard Harry on the phone with the 911 operator. I walked to their van and put a generous amount of super glue on the door handles of the front doors I emptied the rest on the handle of the sliding side door.

I then walked to the back of the van, withdrew my gun, and waited. I didn't have to wait very long. There was a bunch of yelling and screaming coming from the front of the Walmart store and the three men ran to the van. One of the men was carrying a blond headed girl who was kicking and screaming as he carried her to the van.

All three men reached the van at about the same time, reached for, and then opened the doors and then became frozen in place. Not frozen, but definitely stuck. I walked out from the back of the van, took the little girl away from the big man and I held her until a woman ran up to me and took her daughter out of my arms.

Mrs. Sweet ran up to me and I told her the kids were safe in the truck, she ran to go see for herself.

The men pulled furiously trying to get their hands loose from the van's door handles, but they were stuck solid. There were a bunch of people gathered outside looking at what was going on. Several people were recording this capture on their cell phones. To calm the crowd down I showed them my Sheriff's deputy badge.

"Funny thing about super glue," I said. "It isn't even sticky when it is exposed to air, but let the glue lose contact with the air, like covering it with a hand, it is instantly bonded. You can probably pull your hands off the handles, but you will leave a good portion of your hand on the van. I would then have to shoot you."

A minute later we could hear sirens coming from all directions converging on Walmart. I returned my handgun to its holster, thanking God I didn't have to use it but also, thankful it was available if I had needed it. The police rounded up the onlookers so the detectives could get statements about what they saw. The police sergeant came up to me and said, Le Roy what is going on.

"Well Austin, these 3 yahoos kidnapped a young girl a couple of weeks ago in Mississippi. We stumbled on her in a home in Wetumpka in a hidden room that was part of the underground railroad. They had that little girl taped up like an Egyptian mummy. Do me a favor and call the sheriff and ask him to meet us here. "

"I am sure he is on his way, I heard him respond over the police band, the police officer said. The state police are on their way too. We are going to have quite a party sorting this one out. Did you make a citizen's arrest Le Roy he asked. Oh no. Burt deputized me a couple of days ago. I showed him my badge.

"That was quite a trick super gluing their hands to the van doors." One of the police officers wanted to know how we get their hands unstuck from the van door handles so we can put handcuffs on them and take them to jail?

"Go into Walmart and tell them you are going to need some nail polish remover with acetone in it, a couple of bottles of water and some liquid soap," I said.

He looked at his Sergeant who nodded and went into Walmart with his shopping list.

CHAPTER 62

Just then Sheriff Burt showed up and examined the three men and their sticky situation. "Le Roy, you never cease to amaze me. It's going to take us a good couple of hours to process the scene and get these three locked up. How about Austin, and I stop over after and get everyone's statements. No reason to keep the kids here. I'm sure they would rather be swimming in your pool than to be here in the Walmart parking lot."

I nodded in agreement and headed to my truck.

I climbed back in the truck, and it was filled with laughter. "What is so funny," I asked

Mrs. Sweet's face turned all red and she said, "with all the excitement at the front of the store I ran out to check on Kathy and the boys and ran out without paying for Kathy's new bathing suit.

Harry said, "she is the new public enemy number 1." At that we all had a good laugh. Don't worry, you can come back and pay them tomorrow.

We headed back home; the boys and Kathy couldn't wait to tell Judy all about the excitement that had just taken place at the Walmart parking lot.

I told her that Austin and Burt would be over after a while to get statements from everyone.

Mrs. Sweet called her husband and filled him in on what had happened in the Walmart parking lot. He and the realtor cut the house visitation for the day short, and they headed back to the house. I phoned Dr. Lee and updated her on today's events. I told her that it seems the capture of the kidnappers had fixed something that was keeping Kathy from remembering about the kidnapping. How she had all kinds of details she was willing to share. Dr. Lee said her husband had just arrived home and she had been telling him about the past few days.

I told her to pack him, the Duchess, and Duke and come over for supper. We have plenty, don't worry about bringing anything.

I sent the boys to go pick some sweet corn for supper. Kathy and her dad joined them in the garden to help. Mrs. Sweet was helping Judy whip something up in the kitchen while I got "Old Smoky" ready to fire up.

I grabbed a stack of frozen burgers from the freezer, added some pecan pellets to "Old Smoky" and in about 15 minutes laid the ears of corn on the grill to start them roasting. When the corn was just about done, I added the burgers to the grill, seasoned them up with a little liquid steak seasoning, onion, and garlic powders. Abby watched me intently hoping that I was also cooking her a couple of those burgers or at the very least would drop a couple.

Dr. Lee, her husband Rich, and the Duke and the Duchess arrived. Dr. Lee did not come empty handed she brought a big platter of deviled eggs. Soon everyone had a seat at the table, we joined hands, and said a very special prayer of thanks. I am not sure how GOD did it, but he had a plan, and it sure worked out well. Just as we were starting to eat, both the local and state police sergeants and the Sheriff showed up to take our statements. They saw we were eating supper and tried to back out until we were done. I told them I had already cooked them burgers too and invited them to join us. They looked at each other and at the plate of hamburgers, grabbed a plate and joined us.

Kathy remarked, "This town sure is a friendly place look at all the friends I have made in just two days." Everyone laughed.

Just as we finished supper out comes Judy with strawberry shortcake for dessert. What a great ending to a good meal.

Mr. & Mrs. Sweet said, "We can't thank everyone enough for the roles they played in rescuing Kathy and we are so glad that nightmare is behind us."

CHAPTER 63

Burt said, "I'm afraid we have a lot more to accomplish and not a whole lot of time to do it.

"What do you mean," Mrs. Sweet asked.

Burt said, "It is obvious that your daughter was not the first one to be kidnapped by these three monsters. They are a part of a much bigger organization that has been trafficking young girls like your daughter. More than likely Kathy is not the only one, nor the first child that they have kidnapped. There are more, perhaps a lot more, kids like Kathy who didn't end up with a happy reunion like she did."

Kathy spoke up, "That's right she said, I remember the list of girl's names written on the wall of the barn I was kept chained in."

The state police sergeant's eyes lit up, "if you could remember the names on that list or help us find that old barn that would be a BIG help."

"I will help in any way I can," Kathy volunteered.

Kathy, her mom, Dr. Lee, the Sheriff, the police chief, and I adjourned to the dining room to attempt to extract as much from Kathy as she was now able to fill in.

She remembered that they had put her in a white van that didn't have any windows in the back or sides. She remembered the three names or probably nick names of the three men who had taken her, Snake, Hoss, and Speedy. She told of being taken to a convenience store where she was allowed to use the bathroom and they fed her, but she had no idea where that store was located. She knew the old lady she had met was the kidnappers' mother, but that's all she could remember. The law enforcement team who once looked hopeful now looked disappointed.

Dr. Lee spoke up and said, "there may be another way to help Kathy remember."

All eyes turned towards her.

She said, "we could try hypnosis."

Mrs. Sweet looked frightened and said, "you want to hypnotize my little girl? Hasn't she been through enough?"

"I assure you it is perfectly safe." Dr. Lee said.

"I want to talk this over with my husband before we decide." She left the room and went out on the deck to talk it over

with her husband.

While they were outside the Sheriff updated the rest of us to what was going on behind the scenes. "The three brothers had been arrested and isolated from one another. Separate interrogations were taking place. They have been fingerprinted and we are confident that these three have broken the law before. We will soon have their real names and some history on them. But right now, none of them are talking. Today is Saturday, which means they won't be brought before a judge and officially charged with kidnapping until Monday morning. That is a lucky break because that gives us tonight and tomorrow to build a tighter case that these snakes can't wiggle out of."

The Sweet's reentered the dining room to ask a few more questions about the possible hypnosis of their daughter only to hear the Sheriff say, "Le Roy It was a huge benefit that you caught them in the process of kidnapping another child. If it wasn't for that, the kidnapping of Kathy may not have been enough to hold them over for trial."

Everyone looked in utter disbelief.

"How could that possibly be?" Mr. Sweet asked.

The Sheriff said, "Our forensic team has yet to turn up any physical evidence tying them to the kidnapping of Kathy. It seems like they steam cleaned the entire inside of the van so there is no trace of Kathy's DNA to prove she was ever in that van. That plus it would be the testimony of three adults vs. one 10-year-old traumatized little girl.

They would look at Dr. Lee as a mental health professional that was required to help stabilize Kathy. You never know how a jury will react. Fortunately, Le Roy, you caught them in the act. Unfortunately, although quite amusing any defense attorney worth a hill of beans would find a way to twist the unconventional method you used to capture those three as cruel and unusual."

"We need some physical evidence to prove beyond a shadow of a doubt Kathy's description of what happened can be verified."

"That can only come from her and right now she doesn't consciously remember."

CHAPTER 64

Mr. & Mrs. Sweet asked if they could be present while their daughter was under hypnosis.

Dr. Lee said, "Once she is under hypnosis you are welcome to observe but until she is under your presence may make it difficult for her to achieve a total hypnotic state."

She then asked the Sheriff what questions he needed answers to. The police joined him in making a list, then the room cleared out except for Dr. Lee and Kathy. Dr. Lee dimmed the lights and talked softly to Kathy encouraging her to relax. It took about 15 minutes before Kathy was deeply hypnotized. Dr. Lee went to the door and let the Sweet's and the sheriff enter the room reminding them they were to observe only, no talking. They nodded in agreement.

The Dr. took her back to the morning of her kidnapping. She asked her where she ate breakfast that morning and she replied Waffle House. She then asked what she had eaten for breakfast that morning and she said a pecan waffle and three slices of bacon. She then asked her about the tour bus and Kathy remembered the guys from the VFW, Mary Jane, the tour guide, and she even remembered the bus drivers name was Ralph and how that also was another word for throwing up.

She knew all about going to see the home where Elvis was born and that they hit the Blues Trail. She was able to remember stopping at the Blue Front Café. She remembered what her family had all ordered for lunch and all the famous autographed guitars hanging on the walls. She then remembered telling her parents she was going outside to get some pictures of the front of the cafe with the camera of her new cell phone. She remembered a guy asking her if she wanted him to take her picture. She had said, "yes," and the next thing she knew someone had put a bag of some kind over her head, she had felt a prick in her upper arm and then falling asleep. During this last statement Kathy's breathing had changed and she was starting to show signs of duress. Dr. Lee calmed her back down ensuring her that she was completely safe. Kathy was able to remember the name of the convenience store they had taken her to.

Kathy shared that she had been shackled in an old barn, and the old lady that lived on the place had told her that the kidnappers were her sons. She had also told her that the kidnapping ring was using the stations which were once used by the underground railroad as a method to transfer abducted kids, from one city to another. The woman also shared that her boys worked for her husband, and he was always on the road, but that her boys could always get time off when they needed it to come see their momma and to transport little girls like me.

Kathy remembered that their mom liked to use a bull whip and promised Kathy, she would use it on her if she heard so much as a peep up at the house. The woman had demonstrated her expertise by killing some of the rats that made the barn their home. Kathy told them that it seemed like the mother was in charge and that her 3 sons feared her. The hypnosis was even able to help Kathy remember the names on the wall behind a bale of straw.

Dr. Lee stopped the hypnosis and put her into a deep sleep. When she awoke from the hypnosis, Kathy said, that she felt very good. She was sent outside to see what the boys were doing. The law enforcement team reentered the dining room and listened to the tape Dr. Lee had recorded of the hypnosis session. They were all scribbling down notes and making a plan.

"This is big, really big," said the Sheriff. "This is a whole lot bigger than just one case of kidnapping and child trafficking. It obviously includes Mississippi, Alabama, and Georgia. As much as I hate to say this, we need the power of the FBI if we are going to shut down this whole child trafficking pipeline across 3 states. They have the resources and the clout to handle something this big, especially when it goes across the state lines."

CHAPTER 65

The problem with that is once the bureau gets involved it becomes their show. This is a time when we must move fast. It is the only way we can rescue the kids already in the pipeline. Another thing that really concerns me is that I find it impossible for something this big to be taking place right under our noses without the help of authorities. There have got to be some crooked cops in on this. If we put this out through our channels it is bound to alert them, and they will close shop.

I spoke up, "Couldn't you call the FBI after we had things covered?"

The Sheriff said, "Yes, but there is a problem with manpower. Without the FBI we are dead in the water. We just don't have the manpower for something like this, and even if we did, word would leak out."

"I think I have a solution for your manpower issue," I said. Let me make a couple of calls first.

The Sheriff called his connection at the FBI, and explained what they believed was taking place. The FBI agent said he would put together a response team and be there first thing in the morning.

The Sheriff believed that Kathy had provided the information that might make one of the three kidnappers break their silence.

I looked at my wife and she said, "you have done enough; I know you feel like they have left you out of the rest of the case but there is nothing more you can do."

"I have an idea that may make a difference. Do you have Kristie's number?

"Yes, it's in my phone, what do you want to call her for?" Judy wanted to know.

"I need her to unlock the historical society and let the boys and I in. We have some research that we must get done before morning. It could be the difference between life or death or at the very least a life of captivity."

I spoke to Kristie on the phone and when I told her what I was up to she was only too willing to help. She said she would meet us there in 15 minutes.

The boys and I hopped in the truck and got to the historical society just as Kristie was opening the door. We went right to work. I asked Kristie for a map of the town to start with. We taped it to a bulletin board and Kristie was able to give us a box filled with different color push pins. She dragged out the big book she had on the underground railroad.

I told her I was looking for places that had been underground railroad stations. As I read off the street addresses the boys put a red push pin in the map. If a place was more likely than not suspected of being part of the underground railroad, it received a yellow push pin. When we had finished, there were 22 red and 7 yellow pins in just our county.

Kristie, said, "I had no idea there were that many locations in the county."

I then asked her, if she could contact the historical society managers in the neighboring counties and ask them to do the same exercise for their counties, we need it before first light.

I looked at the map and said, "I wish there was some way we could put all of this data in one place so we could sort it."

Child Trafficking and the Underground Railroad

Harry spoke up and said, "I can do that grandpa, I'll just put it in an excel spread sheet that way we can easily sort it."

Kristie got Harry into the computer and Shane started reading off the list of locations while Harry entered them into Excel, whatever that is.

I called the Sheriff, "and asked him to swing by the historical society," I think I have a good idea. Fifteen minutes later the Sheriff showed up.

He said, "I sure hope this idea is better than the one where you used super glue to capture three kidnappers. I am still getting phone calls about that asking if it is true and is it the new and approved method of securing prisoners in my county."

"Burt, never argue with success," I said.

CHAPTER 66

I showed him the map. He whistled, "I had no idea there were that many locations in my county. Obviously, I did not pay enough attention in history class."

I said, "historians believe that during the civil war and the years leading up to it over 100,000 people used this underground railroad to freedom. To transfer that many people in twos and threes it would take a lot of stations."

At 9:00 the data from the other counties started pouring in and Harry added them to the data base. When this exercise was completed, we had a map of a four-county area with forty-seven red and yellow stick pins.

The sheriff said, "okay, you have a map of four counties with all different color stick pins."

I said, "Yes, and these stick pins represent known or suspected locations of stops along the underground railroad. We know that the kidnappers are using underground railroad stations as a haven for transporting kidnapped kids. I suggest we visit each one, tonight and see what we find. I am betting it will turn up several kids that are in the middle of being moved to some of these locations. If there is no one at these locations, we leave a deputy there for say 12 hours and see what we catch."

"Le Roy," the sheriff said, "for a minute let's say your idea makes sense, and I am not saying it does. You know I only have 12 deputies and we patrol the entire county. Where would we get the manpower to search all these sites? To do it safely, and that is the only way I would do it, you would need two men dedicated to each of these stations. They would have to be willing to stay there the entire night. With my force that means we could only visit six of those sites in my county. Where are we going to get that kind of manpower, the national guard?"

"No, not the national guard, but you are close." I told him my idea.

While shaking his head from side to side, he said, "you know that might just work. If this doesn't turn up a single child being trafficked or a single trafficker, I am going to be the laughingstock of the county and maybe the entire state. I can forget about running for reelection. What are the Sheriffs in my neighboring counties going to say when they find out how I have overstepped my boundaries and started an operation in their county without so much as a phone call."

"If I am right, I interrupted, those neighboring sheriffs will start getting phone calls and will be too busy answering questions from the press to worry about it. In the end they will be thanking you. I need to make a couple of phone calls."

Burt said, "I guess we should talk about which of the sites my deputies should be sent to."

I shook my head and said, "none of them."

He looked in disbelief, then asked, "why not, they are the most qualified for an operation like this."

"Burt, I hate to be the bearer of bad news, but you yourself brought up the likelihood that if there has been this much trafficking going on right under your nose and the other sheriff's noses that some law enforcement had to be involved."

"None of my men," Burt stated. "I would trust every one of them with my life."

I said, "If that is the case, none of them will get caught up in our nets tonight. Then you will know for sure."

CHAPTER 67

Burt and I rode in his sheriff's car, with the boys in the back seat.

Harry said, "this is neat, we look like real prisoners."

We drove to the VFW building. The parking lot was full of cars. There were more cars than on Bingo night.

We entered the building, there were at least eighty veterans and legionnaires there. The sheriff shook hands with the commanders of both posts and asked the men to sit down.

He walked up to the podium and turned on the microphone. He said, "everyone in this room has served his country in the past. I'm asking you to serve our state and our county tonight. We have a serious problem with human traffickers, right here in our own back yard. I don't have enough men to check all the locations. We apprehended three suspects in the middle of a kidnapping attempt at our Walmart yesterday. We feel that the rest of the traffickers will try to push as many kidnap victims as possible through pipeline before they are forced to shut it down. They are using the old underground railroad locations to move them. I am not using my men or the deputies in any of the surrounding counties because of the remote possibility there might be some law enforcement people involved. This will be the largest sting operation in the state. If you choose not to take part, I will fully understand. I would be lying to you if I said there was no personal risk, and I won't do that. If anyone chooses to leave, please do so now and I will spare you the details."

Not a man got up to leave. "Okay let's get started. Until further notice every man in this room is now deputized. When your commanders were contacted, they chose you because they believed each of you were authorized to carry a weapon and that you had sufficient training while you were in the service. You were also felt to be the best men for the job. Does every man here have a permit to carry? Is there anyone here who is not carrying?" Not a single hand was raised. "Gotta love the second amendment and the state of Alabama."

"There will be three of you assigned to each location. As soon as you arrive do a quick sweep of the location. You may find a kidnap victim and you may find a kidnapper. If you find a victim, call either me or Le Roy and we will retrieve. If you find any adult you are to place them under arrest, even law enforcement, frisk them, and detain them. Plastic handcuffs will be issued to you. If no one is there one of you stay. The other two take up surveillance positions. Stay in touch with your team with your cell phones. If you do arrest someone fill out a 5x7 card, write down who, when, and where, print your name, sign your name, and put your cell phone numbers on the card. My and Le Roy's cell phone number is on the board. Make sure you add it to your contacts in your phone. If you have a prisoner, call one of us. The Army reserve unit on Parker Avenue has volunteered to provide a paddy wagon and take care of temporarily holding the suspects in their stockade. We can sort it all out in the morning."

Burt said, "Do not tell anyone else what is taking place, not your wives, girlfriends, or wives and girlfriends. Laughter rang out and lightened the mood."

"If possible, no shootouts. We don't want to risk anyone getting injured or killed. If anyone must discharge their weapon the entire operation has failed and our chances of saving a kid from a life of slavery has ended."

"One final warning there is the remote possibility that someone from law enforcement might be involved. You are to treat them as if they were one of the kidnappers.

"Any questions?" One hand shot up, "Yes," the Sheriff said. The man stood up and asked the sheriff if he knew what the word Navy stood for. The sheriff shook his head and said, "no I'm sorry I don't."

"Never Again Volunteer Yourself." Everyone laughed.

CHAPTER 68

One of the commanders took the microphone back and announced that once the sting operation was over the VFW and Legion auxiliaries would be serving breakfast for all of them.

The men fell into groups of three and were given their assignments.

I said, "Now came the hard part, the waiting."

We didn't have to wait long for the first call. Two men were apprehended as they attempted to remove a bound girl from the basement of a house on Franklin Street.

Dr. Lee was contacted. She drove to the VFW. There were two children who had been rescued awaiting her care. She got on the phone and called all the psychologists that she knew. She had them call the counselors that they knew and soon she had more mental health professionals helping than they had patients. Before the night was out that would all change.

Despite being told to keep this hush hush it was obvious that word had spread to the Navy and Air Force reserve centers as they dispatched corpsman, first responders, and medical staff of Dr's and nurses to provide any medical assistance that might be required.

The Sheriff contacted the mayor, district attorney, and the news desk at the local newspaper. The mayor told the Sheriff not to do anything until he and the district attorney showed up, the Sheriff told him it was too late, men were already at their assigned areas.

When the mayor arrived, he was madder than a wet hornet. His face was all red and he started firing questions left and right at the Sheriff, never giving him a chance to answer before shooting another question at him.

The mayor asked, "Just who came up with this crazy idea that kidnappers were using the old underground railroad, was it you?"

The Sheriff shook his head and said, "the man you want to thank is Le Roy and his grandsons. They were the ones who rescued that kidnap victim the other day in the Walmart parking lot. They captured the three suspects that had delivered a kidnap victim, and they also figured out the criminals were using the old underground railroad as a method to move their captives. They identified the locations and together we set up a plan, to perform a sting operation in ours and three neighboring counties."

The mayor's face got so red it looked as if it were going to explode. "You mean you listened to this old loon who goes around with crazy glue and glues people to their car door handles? You mean that loon?"

"Sure is Mr. Mayor, one and the same, and his name is Le Roy Cristman. Instead of trying to belittle him you should be thanking him. He appears to be the only one who has seriously put a dent in the child trafficking rings that are running rampant through many of the southern states."

"Did you know my office is still getting phone calls about that unorthodox method of securing prisoners. You do know the first thing those defense lawyers are going to bring up is that he was a civilian that had overstepped his bounds. He superglued their hands to their van door and threatened them with a loaded weapon. We are going to be the laughingstock of the county, the state, and maybe the entire country."

"I had lawfully deputized him the day before when he volunteered to not only provide a safe haven for that little girl and her parents but provide protection to her while she tried to get back some normalcy in her life. That action allowed me to free up two additional deputies because we didn't need to provide security for her and her family."

"I am sure you got the Sheriffs in the neighboring counties to go along with this crazy plan."

"No sir." the sheriff, said, "I acted alone."

"You decided? What do you mean you decided? This isn't for you to decide." The mayor said, "you mean you have our people doing this crazy stuff in other counties?"

"I decided there wasn't time to go through proper channels. I have been a big believer in better to act now and beg for forgiveness later. Lives were at stake," the sheriff responded.

"Where did you get the manpower to do all this?" the mayor asked.

"That was my idea, to use members of the American Legion and the VFW to visit each of the sites and take appropriate action if warranted," the Sheriff responded.

"You mean you sent our citizens into harm's way not just in our county but the neighboring counties? Why would they go along with such a request. On whose authority?"

"Mine," the sheriff said, "I deputized them first."

The mayor said, "You can be sure the first thing tomorrow I am having an emergency meeting of the city council and asking them to take your badge." You will no longer have to worry about deputizing half the town of old folks to act as your private army.

As soon as the mayor told the sheriff that he was through in his town. It got quiet, real quiet.

CHAPTER 69

Then the phones started ringing. Each commander answered a phone and announced how many kids rescued and how many suspects were taken into custody.

The boys kept score on a white board. Just when the calls started to die off from the people sent out in our county calls started coming in from the other counties in the sting operation.

We had kidnapped victims coming in from most of the locations identified with the push pins. Not a single report of any shooting. The local national guard reported they had sixty-four men in custody in their stockade.

The mayor and the sheriff began calling their counterparts in the other counties. Most of them blew their tops when they found out that Bert had orchestrated a sting operation under their noses in their counties with no warnings. Burt let them vent for a few minutes before reading off the 5x7 cards, the notes about who had been arrested from their county. All the bluster left them when they were informed that at least one deputy in each county had been caught trying to help the traffickers.

The sheriff said, "that had we gone through normal channels the first thing we would have done is told our deputies and these raids would have been for nothing. No arrested traffickers and more importantly no 32 rescued victims would have been discovered. Don't feel bad, one of my own deputies was caught up in this sting."

What really won them over to sheriff Burt's way of thinking was when he told them they had arrested sixty-four traffickers and once the paperwork was complete, they could pick them up at the national guard's detention center. "Think of it like curb side pickup."

The mayor and the prosecutor could not believe the success of the sting operation. It had freed thirty 32 kidnap victims and netted arresting 67 suspects including 4 local law enforcement, 2 state police, a state congressman, and even a judge. They all seemed to have been involved in the trafficking enterprise.

The local reporter who had just arrived on the scene spoke up," Mr. Mayor, this story is going to make national news. It will be all over the network news, CNN, MSNBC, and Fox will all want interviews. Mayor your town is going to get big time exposure the way his Sheriff's department was on top of all these kidnappings. Are you sure you want to fire the Sheriff that is a hero to 360 million people?"

"Perhaps I did act too quickly" I will contact the governor's office and he will want to be here and probably give me an award for the great job in breaking this major child trafficking ring." The mayor said.

The mayor patted the sheriff on the back and telling him what a great detective job he had done in assisting him in breaking up this trafficking ring.

The evening Telegram reporter just shook his head as he noted all the exchanges.

CHAPTER 70

I checked on my grandsons. They were sound asleep on the couch in the commander's office.

I too was exhausted and wished I could join them on the couch for 40 winks. At 66 I am not as young as I was when this whole thing started four days ago. The Sheriff and I sat down across from each other and had some breakfast the ladies' auxiliaries had prepared.

"So, what's next for you Le Roy? You and your grandsons going to open your own detective agency?"

"No," I just chuckled. I think I am going to head to the house sleep for about two days straight, wake up, eat something and then hibernate for the rest of the week.

Your grandsons are very special young men. "Do you get to see them very often?"

"I am going to have to send my grandsons back home in a couple of weeks, they must start school and I am sure their parents miss them."

I told him about the 10-year-old rule when my children had to send me their children for the summer. I have two more grandsons in the pipeline in four more years that will turn 10 and spend the summer with the wife and me. After that I will have done my part in raising them to be good citizens and hopefully, taught them some life lessons that will come in handy as they get older, just as my grandfather did for me, and I imagine his grandfather did for him."

"What is so special about 10 years old? Why not 12 or 13?"

"I have never told anyone this before and I am counting on you keeping it a secret. He nodded. "The summer I turned 10 was the last time I saw my grandfather. He died of a massive heart attack. I like to believe I learned life lessons from him at 10 years old that have lasted my entire life. Ten years old is the perfect age to mold a young mind. They are old enough to remember what you teach them, old enough to be able to reason, and more importantly they aren't teenagers."

Burt just laughed. He said, "Le Roy before you hibernate, I have one prisoner I must interview, and I thought you might enjoy the first part of the interview."

We each picked up a drowsy little boy and carried them to the back seat of the truck. We drove to the detention compound at the national guard center. There was a soldier standing outside who said she would keep an eye on my grandsons as they slept in the back seat of my truck. I told her I shouldn't be long.

The Sheriff must have phoned ahead because the suspect he wanted to interview was waiting for us in an interview room.

These places with jail cells have always given me the creeps. Hearing that metal door close behind you just scares me.

I took one look at the person handcuffed to the interview table and I said, "Why am I not surprised?" The first thing the Sheriff did was inform him of his rights and tell him this interview was being recorded.

Seargent Larry Phillips, of the Alabama state police, demanded to be released this instant. That he had been illegally taken hostage by a couple of old men with guns. They had caught him alright, just as he was about to release one of the kidnap victims. He claimed to be following up on clues he had uncovered during his off-shift time.

"Let me see if I have this right," the Sheriff said. "You just happened to stumble on some clues leading you to the old mill on

Prescott Street. You just happened to know there was a kidnap victim there, only she was gone by the time you arrived. Is that correct."

"Exactly," he said.

"That's the reason you had changed out of uniform too, right? I bet if your little plan had worked you would be claiming overtime," the Sheriff said.

The sheriff said, "there are a lot of holes in your story Phillips and the deeper we start looking at you the more and deeper those holes are going to become. I suggest you think of some better lies before you are brought before the judge on Monday morning.

"I already know that even from the beginning you had lied to us. You never, just happened to be driving back from Mississippi after delivering a prisoner, and just accidentally had your police band on your radio tuned into the Mississippi highway patrol. There was no prisoner transfer to Mississippi that morning. I know because I checked. You knew about the upcoming kidnapping of Kathy Sweet because the three Stone brothers worked for you."

"As soon as we find the barn that held kidnapped victims that will round up just about everything. You also never put out an amber alert for Kathy Sweet. We checked Snakes phone and guess who he had numerous calls to and from on his phone's history log. None other than yours. I have more than enough evidence on you to get a warrant. The state has some of the best forensic accountants who will dig into your and your family's finances so deep they will be able to tell if you bought lemonade at a kid's lemonade stand."

"Do you have anything you'd like to add Sergeant Phillips?"

"I'd like a lawyer," he replied.

I spoke up and said, "I should have known how evil you were when you attempted to kick Dr. Lee's dogs." Dogs can sense the evil in somebody."

CHAPTER 71

The Sheriff and I had become very close in the past few days. I told him he had done an excellent job.

"I am thinking when the evening news paper comes out it will have the full exchange between you and our mayor for the entire town to read. I believe you will win the next election in a landslide. The mayor not so much," I added.

"Le Roy, I think you should run for mayor. With the good press you are going to get from this escapade you will be a shoe in. The town could use a good mayor for a change," the Sheriff stated.

"What? Who me? I don't like politics, and I don't like politicians. Besides I'm already retired, twice, "I said.

"No, not me, never had liked politics very much, besides it would interfere with my FEAS."

"What does FEAS stand for? I never heard of it before." The Sheriff asked.

It stands for Fishing, Eating, AND Sleeping. The sheriff laughed as we shook hands and said goodbye.

I drove the boys back home and as we pulled into the drive; we saw a welcoming party waiting for us. My bride Judy, Mr. & Mrs. Sweet and Kathy, Dr. Lee and her husband; the Duke and the

Duchess, and of course Abby. The three dogs' tails were wagging so hard, I thought they might fall off.

Kathy told the boys to get their bathing suits on, the last one in the pool is a rotten egg. The three of them took off to get changed.

We went out to the pool to watch over the kids.

I updated everyone on what had taken place last night, the arrests made, and the girls saved.

Dr. Lee mentioned that she had been in contact with most of the girls' parents and set up a group therapy meeting with the girls. Since they had all been through a similar experience it may help the girls open up more if Kathy could join them in these sessions.

Kathy was on the way to the pool when she heard her name come up. Dr. Lee explained that she would like her to help with the therapy for the other kidnap victims. Kathy said she was more than willing to help in any way she can.

Dr. Lee said, "The sooner they can come to the realization that this was a bad experience, but it is over, and they can move on, the faster they will recover. It is going to take a while, but you can see for yourself the great strides Kathy has made to normalcy."

Mr. & Mrs. Sweet had good news to share as well. They had found a house to buy. Not only was it in their neighborhood, but just around the corner.

Kathy said, "By moving that close it solves three problems at once."

"What might those problems be young lady?" I asked.

"Well," she said. "Harry and Shane will be leaving very soon to go back with their families. My closest grandparents live in Texas, which is way too far away, and you and I can have more adventures together. So, it's all settled I am officially your new granddaughter. Besides you are going to need some help when you run for mayor."

"What is this running for mayor thing all about?" Judy said.

Kathy said, "The boys told her the Sheriff said you should run for mayor and that you would be a shoe in, especially after what was going to be in today's paper."

I thought the boys were fast asleep when Burt was flapping his jaws. I never said I was running for mayor.

Child Trafficking and the Underground Railroad

Judy said, "You should do it. It will get you out of my house during the week and at the same time give you something to do."

"But I have my garden, my shop, my fishing trips." I countered.

"Sounds a lot like me, me, and me. Don't you ever think of anyone but yourself? People in this town need an honest mayor for a change," Judy replied. "God has given you so many talents. It would be sinful if you didn't put those talents to good use."

"You certainly have our vote," Mrs. Sweet chirped in.

"I am no politician, I hate politics," I spoke.

"All the more reason why you should run, maybe what this country needs are fewer politicians," Mr. Sweet interjected.

Mrs. Sweet added, "You have a lot of good qualities that people should look for in their elected officials."

"I prefer to work behind the scenes."

"After the home-runs you hit this week, people are going to stand up and take notice."

"That's enough of that nonsense," I said. "I think I am going to go take a nap."

I was in a deep sleep when I heard a racket out on the front porch. I headed out there and found that everyone had their heads buried in the Evening Telegram newspaper.

What is everyone oohing about? I wanted to know.

Judy spoke up and said, "According to the paper you should run for governor or even president of the United States."

There are quotes here from Dr. Lee, Sheriff Kaper, the police chief, and even Kathy was interviewed. They told the story how first you rescued Kathy, then single handedly out witted her three kidnappers in the Walmart parking lot rescuing another just captured girl. No mention of you using unconventional apprehension techniques. How you are the one that tied the kidnappers to the old underground railroad stations. Your fast actions saved 32 previously kidnapped young girls and saved them from a life of slavery. Arresting 67 suspects in the process. You identified corruption in 4 counties and the local government.

Our current mayor is toast because he points out in the paper and I quote, "Our current mayor had all but fired the Sheriff until he learned about the success of the sting operation, and then tried to take all the credit."

"Looks like you will have clear sailing in your bid for the mayor's job." Judy stated.

I just shook my head and said, "I will think about it." Evidently my saying I would think about it meant a definite yes to my wife. When next I looked up there was a crowd gathering on my front lawn. There must have been 50 people there and they were all clapping.

CHAPTER 72

Judy couldn't wait to post on Facebook to all our friends and neighbors that I was leaning toward running for Mayor. Then the phone started to ring, and ring, and ring some more. CNN and MSNBC wanted to fly me to NY to be interviewed. Next Fox news called and said they would fly someone here to interview me.

I had to get away and asked the grandsons and my newest granddaughter if they wanted to go try and catch some catfish for supper. They ran to get their fishing poles, but I told them to forget about using worms today. Today we would be using crickets. Crickets are much better this time of day.

"Why is there an apple in the cricket cage?" Shane asked.

"The crickets will eat the cut-up apple I put in there. It gives them food and moisture to drink. The thing about crickets that many people don't know is that if you don't give them something to eat when they get hungry, they just start eating each other."

"Yuck," said Kathy. "I could have gone my entire life without learning that fact."

"That makes them cannibals," Shane chimed in with.

Harry entered the conversation and said, "people do it too."

"No way." said Kathy. "That is only in the jungle or made up for movies."

I said, "Kathy, "history tells us Harry is correct. In the spring of 1846, a group of nearly 90 emigrants left Springfield, Illinois, and headed west. Led by brothers Jacob and George Donner, the group attempted to take a new and supposedly shorter route to California. They were taking this new route because someone told them it was faster. Nothing could have been further from the truth. They got up high in the mountains and got trapped by a huge snowstorm. Due to the delays, they had run out of food. Almost 90 people started that trip and fewer than 50 walked out. There was only one thing available to eat and give those 50 a chance to survive. That one thing unfortunately was each other. The group was forced to cannibalism to survive and finish the journey to California the following year. When reduced to cannibalism to survive through the winter, only half of the original group reached California the following year. Their story quickly spread, and before long the term "Donner Party" became synonymous with one of humanity's most ingrained taboos."

"Can we please talk about something else?" asked Kathy.

Shane said, "if crickets eat apples what keeps the worms alive?"

"They eat coffee grounds. Neither your grandmother nor I drink coffee so I have asked our neighbors to save them for me. Once a week I go collect the used coffee grounds and feed the worms."

I showed each one of them how to put crickets on their hooks. Once the cricket hit the water and started swimming a catfish came to the surface and inhaled it.

It wasn't long and we had enough fish for everyone when Harry spoke up and said, "we still need two more."

"This is fun," said Kathy, "I want to catch a lot more."

Shane told her, "You never take more than you need, that would be wasteful."

"Then why the two extras?" Kathy asked.

"When the farmer, Mr. Will is nice enough to let us fish in his catfish pond we always catch him and his wife one too," added Harry.

I just nodded my head; the boys had learned quite a bit this summer.

We got home with our catch, cleaned them and got the outdoor grill, old Smoky, fired up. Judy won't let me cook fish in the house, she says the cooked fish smell stays in the house for weeks.

As soon as the grease was hot enough, I fried up the catfish and by the time they were done the ladies had brought out the salads they had made while we were fishing, we had a feast.

After supper the kids went out to catch lightning bugs and the grownups sat around the table. Judy said, "You must make up your mind if you are going to run for mayor and you must decide tonight."

"Why do I have to decide tonight?"

Because tomorrow is the last day you can throw your hat in the ring and get your name on the ballot. Just so you know that phone hasn't stopped ringing and the callers urging you to run. I took a message for you from Fox news, and they are sending a reporter here for a live interview. They will be here at 6:00 AM.

That means you will have to be up by 4 so I can get the bed made and my make-up on."

"Wait a minute! If the reporter isn't going to be here until 6 why can't I sleep until 5:30.

"You don't want to be all sleepy eyed in front of the camera."

CHAPTER 73

The interview went fine, I agreed to run for Mayor for one four-year term only.

August 7th arrived a whole lot quicker than I had hoped. The boys' families had come to pick them up as promised. Judy and I hugged our boys, they left knowing how much they were loved. Just as they were being loaded up, both boys ran back to me to give me one final hug. Tears cascaded down their cheeks, and mine were watering too. Must have been something in the air.

The boys said thanks for a great summer Grandma and Grandpa. Kathy and the Sweet's showed up too. Kathy handed them each a piece of paper and said, "this is my email address. I better hear from both of you at least once a week."

I have something for all three of you. I handed my grandsons each a check from their savings at the bank they looked at the checks and said, a thousand dollars. That's what you earned running the fruit and vegetable stand this summer. "Kathy since you are going to be staying in town, I left your share in the bank. I do have one thing that I think you have been missing." I handed her a gift that Judy had wrapped for her.

Kathy unwrapped her gift, and her face lit up, it was a Kansas

City Chiefs jersey. She looked closely and saw that it had been signed by Patrick Mahomes the star quarterback of the Kansas City Chiefs and her favorite player.

He had even sent her a letter. It read:

I heard what happened to your last jersey and I gladly replaced it with one of mine. This is my lucky jersey, I wore it in three games, and we won all of them. Hope it brings you luck too. Kathy you rock.

Signed your friend Patrick.

P.S. If you and your parents are ever near a stadium where we are playing give me a call and I will have tickets waiting for you. (560) 932-8999

Tears streamed down her face; You give the best presents ever. You gave me two new wonderful brothers, a set of Grandparents, an adventure I will never forget and now this autographed jersey.

The three grandkids came in for a group hug. Goodbyes were said and tears were shed as the boys went back to their homes.

CHAPTER 74

The FBI did get a hit on the fingerprints of the first kidnappers I had superglued to the van handles. Not surprising this was not their first encounter with the law. They initially had trouble fingerprinting them because the super glue and its removal damaged their fingerprints until the skin grew back.

"Who knew? "I said with a smile.

Even with their fingerprints trying to trace back their address turned out to be a dead end. All three listed their place of employment as their address. That address was the traveling carnival. Although they had been questioned many times by many different interrogators, neither one was willing to give up their mother or admit that their mother had played any role in the kidnapping. Even when offered a reduced sentence they refused to cooperate.

Sheriff Kaper unwilling to give up interviewed each one of them a final time. During the final interview of the one they called Hoss he realized that the boys, or at least Hoss was more scared of his momma than he was going to prison for the next twenty years. He shared with Hoss that if their mother was arrested and it turned out she was the ringleader she would be put in prison for 50 years to life. If Hoss took the plea deal, he would be out of prison long before his mother ever saw the light of day. Hoss looked hopeful but then asked couldn't she get him if they were both in prison together. "Oh no," the Sheriff said, "the women are held in a different prison hundreds of miles from where you would be sent." Hoss's eyes lit up and he said, "where do I sign?"

The district attorney showed up with the plea deal. Hoss signed on the line. He gave up his mom's name she used and the address of the farm. Eight hours later the FBI scrambled their Hostage Rescue Team, and they raided the farm and discovered another kidnapped victim shackled to the post just as Kathy had described. Mrs. Phillips, (her maiden name), had continued to run the trafficking operation even after her boys had been arrested.

The FBI phoned Mr. & Mrs. Sweet and asked if their daughter would be willing to go to Mrs. Phillips farm so she could answer any additional questions that might come up. They asked Kathy if she was up to it, and she said as long as her new grandpa went with her. They called me and of course I said yes.

Sheriff picked us up in his patrol car. I sat in the passenger seat Kathy and her dad in the back. It was very quiet in the car. I was just thinking we needed to say something to break the silence and lighten the mood or this drive to Mississippi was going to be very long indeed. When Sheriff Burt said, "Le Roy I have to ask you but since you are in my patrol car and no longer a deputized sheriff are you carrying a concealed weapon?"

"Now Burt, you should know me better than to ask me a question like that. I reached in my pocket and withdrew a large bottle of crazy glue. I don't leave home without it. Everybody roared. The Sheriff even had to pull off the road he was laughing so hard.

When we got to the farm, they had Mrs. Phillips in handcuffs and in the back of a Mississippi state police car. Kathy hesitantly walked to the barn where she so recently had been enslaved. She held tightly to her dad's and my hands. She walked over to some bales of straw leaning against the wall and pulled them away.

There etched on the covered up section of wall were the list of names of the girls who had been prisoner in the barn before her. Kathy had been able to positively identify Mrs. Phillips as the person

Child Trafficking and the Underground Railroad

who kept her enslaved and had threatened her with a bull whip beating. That was all the Mississippi state police had needed to hear to keep her locked up until trial.

The forensic team hit a home run at the barn, finding numerous places with Kathy's DNA, proving without a shadow of a doubt that she had been held prisoner in that barn.

A crime scene photographer took a picture of the bales of straw and the names in the list. The sheriff leaned over and whispered in my ear that only the bottom five names on the list had been rescued. I nodded.

"Still a lot more to do," he said. "Have you decided if you are going to play an active role or sit on the sidelines."

I told him I had decided last night that I would toss my hat in the ring. He patted me on the back. I said, "I have already got a campaign manager all lined up."

Who might that be he asked.

"Me," said Kathy.

EPILOGUE

Over the next week we heard there have been numerous raids on previously identified underground railroad safe houses across the south. Each were known to have been stations on the underground railroad. Fifty additional people, adult women, boys, as well as girls, had been taken from the traffickers because of those raids. Over 150 men had been taken into custody and charged with trafficking and were now awaiting trial.

The authorities were able to use their data base and look up the names of those behind the bales of straw. Six of the eleven were saved during the sting operation when they raided the known locations of underground railroad stations. Five are still missing.

In our county over the next few months, the wheels of justice brought all the defendants first to an arraignment and later to trial. The four high profile suspects, all had lawyers and had requested bail. The District Attorney stood up and said, "If it please the court the people request no bail be set for these individuals. The crimes these four have done are such that their freedom is outweighed by the safety of the families of our city and county."

The judge looked down at his notes and said, "Mr. Prosecutor, I tend to agree with you, there will be no bail set for these four. The crimes they are accused of committing makes them a flight risk and I have no doubt they would only attempt to get rid of witnesses.

"I do have a recent opening in my calendar and trial will begin on the 17th of September. The defense attorney looked aghast.

"Judge you can't mean this year, that's only two weeks away."

"I most certainly do, you are dismissed and if I were you, I'd start getting prepared, daylight is burning."

"Yes, your honor."

"That goes for you as well Mr. Prosecutor."

The trials did start on September 17th just as the judge had promised.

Kathy was asked to testify in the cases against Mrs. Phillips and her three sons.

The trials were completed by the twenty ninth of October.

The juries found guilty verdicts for all. Everyone was sentenced to the maximum allowed by law except for Hoss who was given 15 years for cooperating with the prosecution.

Kathy's fears about not fitting in were unfounded. Following the write up about her in the Evening Telegram she became a celebrity in school. Everyone wanted to meet and befriend the girl everyone was calling a hero.

Unfortunately, my bid for mayor was successful. Turns out most of the town was ready for a change in leadership and I won the election by an unheard of 79% of the vote. My first official duty when I took office was to request the state auditors perform a detailed dive into the financials of the town. They were quick to identify several accounting irregularities amounting to several hundred thousand dollars and have turned over their findings to the State's Attorney General's office.

Sheriff Kaper was kept in the loop. He caught the outgoing Mayor heading out of the country just ahead of the warrant for his arrest.

Kathy tells me that my grandsons e-mail her quite often and she enjoys catching up with them. She admitted to me there was only one problem with my two grandsons.

"Problem," I said, "what's the problem."

When they both discovered they would be at your house for Christmas they searched my school web site and found out that we have a winter dance. Both have asked me, and I don't want to hurt either one of their feelings.

Take my advice I said, "tell them both yes!"

She said, "that is a great idea."

They told her their families were going to try and go to their grandfather's house for Christmas. The three were looking forward to reconnecting.

They have also asked her to ask me if I couldn't come up with a little adventure for when they came to visit so they wouldn't get bored. They also asked me to have you search your house and find their video games and send them back.

The End

AFTERWORD

Although this book is a work of fiction our country faces an epidemic of child trafficking. You can help, stay alert be law enforcements eyes and ears in your own communities. The mantra of "SEE SOMETHING SAY SOMETHING" has never been as important as it is with this issue, Parents and grandparents teach your children and grandchildren to stay safe and stay away from strangers. Neighbors watch out for your neighbors. Stay safe out there.

NOTES

Chapter 9

1. https://en.wikipedia.org/wiki/Harriet_Tubman

Chapter 16

1. Iran hostage crisis - Wikipedia

Chapter 18

1. BY SPECTRUM NEWS WEATHER STAFF NATIONWIDE PUBLISHED 2:00 PM ET APR. 11, 2022

ACKNOWLEDGMENTS

In no particular order I would like to thank Mary Ellen Johnston, Mary Jane Dennis, Lee McMichael, and my amazing cover illustrator Natasha Sazonova.

A special thank you goes to Lynessa who kept me focused, eye on the prize, words of encouragement and formatting the final project.

ABOUT THE AUTHOR

Born and raised in a small town in upstate New York by a single parent, aided by two loving grandparents, and two not so loving older sisters but caring sisters.

Went to Herkimer Senior High school, a good high school with great teachers. Upon graduation I joined the US Navy's Nuclear Power program where all the fun began.

During my twenty-year career somehow, I managed to find the time to sail around the world twice get married to the girl back home and raise three wonderful kids that have given me seven of the world's best grandchildren.

Managed to get my BS degree in Nuclear Engineering and an MBA.

Upon retirement I went to work for General Electric Energy and after thirty-two years I was diagnosed with stage four non-Hodgkin's Lymphoma.

Thanks to my wife, family, friends, and chemotherapy I became a survivor.

The aftereffects of the chemotherapy have been brutal and lasting. I am currently a 100% homebound Navy Veteran.

Looking to have additional contact with my grandchildren who are all 12 hours from home I started writing a series of children's books highlighted by my imaginary friend Joey I had growing up. After fifteen books in that series, it was time to try something different.

What you are holding in your hand is that new venture. A fan of American History, I try and combine current events with things of the past.

Bryanmosher.writes@gmail.com